NOOR

DAW Books proudly presents
the novels of Nnedi Okorafor:

WHO FEARS DEATH
THE BOOK OF PHOENIX

BINTI: THE COMPLETE TRILOGY
(Binti | Binti: Home | Binti: The Night Masquerade)

NOOR

NOOR

NNEDI OKORAFOR

DAW BOOKS, INC.
DONALD A. WOLLHEIM, FOUNDER
1745 Broadway, New York, NY 10019
ELIZABETH R. WOLLHEIM
SHEILA E. GILBERT
PUBLISHERS
www.dawbooks.com

First Printing, November 2021
1 2 3 4 5 6 7 8 9

To those who unapologetically accept and
embrace *all* that they are.

Bentley: What is it, Major Lawrence, that attracts you personally to the desert?
Lawrence: It's clean.

—*Lawrence of Arabia*

He who waits will see what is in the grass.

—*Burning Grass,* Cyprian Ekwensi

"There is a whirlwind in southern Morocco, the *aejej,* against which the fellahin defend themselves with knives."

—*The English Patient,* Michael Ondaatje

Ja Ido

I would never do this again. *But for the moment, I survived. I went on.*

I focused my attention beyond the soldiers, out into the open desert, where a Noor (Ultimate Corp's famous enormous wind turbines) sat like the world's most bizarre plant. Harvesting clean energy from one of the world's worst environmental disasters. How poetic. The monstrous thing was about a mile away, where the wind began to roar wildly enough that I could hear it from here. Further into the chaos lived more of these fucking turbines. The evil things generated energy for the evil corporation from the whipping sands of the evil Ja Ido. Most use the language of our colonizers and call the enormous never-ending sandstorm the "Red Eye." As I stood looking at its edge, I felt awe. I kept thinking, This isn't Jupiter. This. Is. Earth.

Two days ago, I'd never have imagined I'd see any of this with my own eyes. In my mind, the Red Eye was a distant near-mythical thing like deep sea creatures or dragons. It wasn't something I thought about often. Who could think about it often and be able to get on with their day?

Its dust will turn your eyes red within moments and kill you within minutes, clogging your nose and mouth, packing your lungs. The Red Eye has occupied miles and miles and miles of Northern Nigeria for nearly thirty years. Right now, its swirling proximity *threatened the sun with its girth. It wasn't a threat to me or him for the moment, though. Today, it was the beast who would watch me be a beast. "I'm not afraid," I whispered to it, knowing it could hear me.*

People actually lived in the Red Eye's belly. People fled there. People who didn't want to be a part of "This day and age" or who wanted to make their own day and age. They survived by using sand-deflecting devices, capture stations and super wells, weather-treated clothes, pure audacity, dust and grit. These were people who'd always been in the desert, even during the nationwide protests and riots, fires, droughts, floods, bloody massacres and global pandemics . . . when it looked like humanity was over. Nomads, herdsman, and desolation dwellers. Generations of people who understood and took issue with the agenda of false demarcations. "Non-Nigerians," more popularly known in southern Nigeria and the rest of Africa as "Non-Issues." If they could live in the belly of the beast, why should I fear that beast looming nearby?

I took a deep breath, letting it rush through my being, slowing my heart rate. I shut my eyes against the nearly blocked out sun, the rhythm in my head beating deep and heavy. It was so bright here, just before the enveloping shade of the storm. In this moment, I relished the dark redness of my blood pumping hard through my eyelids and the talking drum that was so so much like the beat my brother would play on his own drum. His playing used to bring everyone together, told them to come and listen. The rhythm in my head reminded me.

I remembered those wonderful festivals where everyone would put down their phones and tablets and windows and make a circle around him, and he would play and play. Feeding their souls, fortifying them, translating the strength of our ancestors into something we all could consume. In my teens, I could only lie there inside the house, unable to move, straining to hear his music. But I knew, even from out there with all those people listening, my brother was talking specifically to me with his talking drums, pushing me out to distant places to meet with my Ancestors and gods.

I rubbed my temples. My body felt different. From a distance, I heard a howl; something was about to die. Surprisingly, after all that had happened, I was still steady. It hadn't been that long, but things were coming to a head. What a relief. Let it come. The darkness of looming clouds is worse than the storm.

I opened my eyes. I grasped the handle and pushed the cracked glass door. I threw myself into the arms of my fate, as I have been doing for decades. And this time I didn't look back. Because to see him asleep on that old inflatable mattress would break my heart a second time in a matter of days. To meet his eyes and the eyes of the only two of his people he had left would make me weak. So I left them. I stepped outside and looked up. The whole world shivered into a new reality. One I could grasp.

CHAPTER 1

What Kind of Woman Are You?

48 HOURS EARLIER . . .

It was late when I got home. I switched the light on in my bedroom and a startled gecko rushed up my wall and tried to hide near the ceiling. "Oh, not today," I muttered. Then I spent the next hour trying to catch it. Thankfully, the thing escaped out the window. Wall geckos have always bothered me, and the thought of sleeping with one in my bedroom made me angry. On top of this, my headache was back. I knew I wasn't going to sleep well.

I drifted into normal sleep just as the sun was rising. I think. I don't quite remember. I was in my bed facing the window, rubbing my temples. My headache wasn't ready to let up, thumping its drumbeat as if it wanted my spirit to go somewhere else. I was gazing across the Abuja building tops, there was a go-slow in the distance and I remember feeling glad that I didn't have to be in it. These days, I rarely had to travel on the highway, anyway, thanks to the auto shop being only two miles away. My world was comfortably small.

The sunrise was a warm one, the breeze wafting into my open window. I liked the heat; when it was hot, I felt languid, effortless, good. I slept naked, unbothered by mosquitoes. They never seemed to like me. A hawk soared past my apartment window. Or maybe it was a vulture. The beating in my head seemed to surge. "Ah," I groaned, rolling over.

Then I was watching my ex-fiancé Olaniyi's back as he walked out the front door into a lush undulating jungle, a fantastic drum beat rolling up the green, red, and yellow leaves of trees and bushes. I looked up and the sky wasn't really the sky because I was dreaming. It was like looking at a sky that was a blue leaf under a strong microscope and you were zooming and zooming in to see that it wasn't a blue leaf at all; it was millions of blue eyes that made up the leaf. All those eyes were looking at me. And then they weren't blue, they were red, like the eyes of lizards looking. Blinking and looking, blinking and looking.

When *I* blinked, I awoke, my heart pounding and my head aching so badly that I winced. I should have known the day would carry its own basket of strange. I should have known to be prepared. It was Friday, but I should have stayed home.

The auto shop expected me in at eleven AM, so there was time. This would be my first weekend without Olaniyi. He'd come by and taken his things days ago, and when he walked in, he was holding heavy black charm beads in one hand and he refused to look me in the eye. He moved quickly, grabbing his clothes, laptop, chargers, his moldy old books. I said nothing, but inside I was weeping.

Now, fiancé gone, my life plans in unexpected ruin, I intended to spend much of the weekend weeping. I was going to wipe all of him away with a delicious meal of egusi soup heavy with shrimp, beef, and fish, smoothly pounded yam, perfectly fried plantain, sliced sweet mango, a coconut cake and hot tea.

I was going to *not* call any of my friends. I was going to work on a sand repelling device called an "anti-aejej," which a man from up north had brought me to repair. I'd only seen and fixed one, all using guess-work. I was sure I could fix this one, too, and I was excited because I was going to fully understand how it worked. All of this I could do in my spotless incense-scented, quiet roomy apartment with no man I loved staring at me as if I were a demon he'd been jujued into loving.

The evening and then the weekend were mine.

But first, I needed to do some food shopping before work. When I'd lived in Lagos, just getting to the market early would have been a whole morning affair. However, I'd followed my fiancé here to Abuja because a good mechanic (especially one with a cybernetic left arm and thus a hyperdexterous hand) can find work anywhere and a good man is hard to find. And so my life was a different story where I could go to the market in the morning and still make it to work on time.

Abuja was slower, lazier, yes. It's only a few hours' drive from the Red Eye, but a few hours' drive is a long drive when you are just trying to live your life. Despite its relative closeness to the abomination in the north, Abuja was a thriving city that rivaled the fast-paced, clean innovative ones in the south like Lagos, Owerri and New Calabar. And in Abuja, men were less likely to run over a woman like me crossing the street.

Today, I could make it to the market and back before work. I drove, as I always did, and I went to my favorite market, the one that was about a mile away. I knew where everything was. Finding all the ingredients I needed would be easy. They knew me there, too. Or so I thought.

It actually *was* a really warm morning. So my dream was right about *that*, at least. It was also right about the refreshing breeze. I wore no make-up. No earrings. I'd braided my shoulder-length dreadlocks to cover the silver nodule that was the tip of my neural implants. Weeks ago, I'd even dyed my dreadlocks jet-black, so no one questioned how "clean" they were (for some reason, people always thought brown dreadlocks were dirty). And for extra cover, I wore a rose-colored veil over my head. I wore a light but long sleeved green silk top. My skirt was thick, covering my ankles and part of my feet, so neither my legs nor my arms were in view. They shouldn't have caused any trouble.

Granted, by definition, to many Nigerians, I was trouble. Even in Abuja, though it wasn't as rabid as in the south, I was a demon. A witch. An abomination. Priests, reverends, bishops, pastors and imams, holy men all over West Africa said so. To replace an organ or two with cybernetic, 3D-printed, non-human parts was fine. People needed pacemakers, new limbs, skin grafts, etc. But if you were one of those people who *seemed* to be "*more* machine than human" for whatever reason, one of those who "refused to obey the laws of nature and die," you were a demon. I'd seen people like me fall victim to jungle justice in viral videos, murdered (or "shut down" as people liked to joke), attacked in the streets and, in less extreme cases, shunned. We were supposed to die; what we were doing instead of dying wasn't living.

Then there are those who clump all of us into the same group. And when you do that, we all became "those Africans so deeply affected by twisted western ideologies that we're obsessed with perfection and what money can buy." We are cultureless children of the filthy rich corrupt elite class that has nothing better to do but augment our bodies with bullshit just because we can. We aren't *real* Africans, we are the bootlickers of the United States, China, or the Emirates.

People here in Abuja have thought I was the daughter of an

energy tycoon or the mistress of an Ultimate Corp exec simply because of what I am. Me. As if. I just wanted to live my life. As I was. As what I chose. As what I was. I was born and raised in Lagos, like 90 million other people. It's not too much to ask.

Anyway, as I said, most of the men and women in this market *knew* me. This was how I'd learned to live over the years. When you are someone like me, one who is always fighting for herself, against oppression, hate, misunderstanding, fear, you move about the world with care. You seek out those places where people will accept you and you nest there.

Why would I want to force my way into a place that hates me? I don't have time or energy for that. When I moved here with Olaniyi, I tasted the environment. Once I decided it was okay, I gradually let myself come to know this part of Abuja and it came to know me. In this market, for over two years, I'd fixed their cars, repaired their phones, brought people relief, made people *happy*. I thought they understood me. As I thought Olaniyi had. Foolish.

I had a basket and a synth-fiber bag with me. I bought semi-ripe plantain from a man who'd just carried in and set down a bunch in his booth. He was happy to sell to me. He'd laughed after we negotiated the price, saying that I was both fair and a cheat. "I am impressed," he said. "And I'm glad there is only one like you." He had his mobile phone stuck to one of those charge belts and it was showing the days' news. I remember what was on because the man's phone was the size of a book, the volume was high enough for everyone in the cluster of stalls to hear, and the anchorwoman had those thick and braided eyebrows that only people in front of cameras had the nerve to have.

"It was a nightmare here yesterday as four Fulani herdsmen armed to the teeth stormed this small Nigerian village on the edge of the Sahel Desert, pillaging and raping as they went," the anchorwoman said, her braided eyebrows raised dramatically. "For decades, these herdsmen have terrorized peaceful farmers trying to live their lives . . ." Then the man was handing me my bag of plantain. He'd looked me over, chuckled and shook his head. "You're so pretty, but you're too tall."

I rolled my eyes and shrugged. "Can't be everything," I said, turning away. I lengthened my cybernetic legs, making myself a little taller as I walked away. My ex hated when I did that. The plantain seller thought I was out of earshot, but I heard him add, "See this demon disguised as a woman. May Allah help us all." Some of the men around him laughed. It wasn't the bad kind of laughter. I knew what the bad kind of laughter sounded like. So I merely rolled my eyes. He'd had one of those blue Imam Shafi Abdulazeez event flyers tacked to the booth wall behind him; they had the image of the imam pointing a finger dramatically upward as he spoke and at the bottom a circle and slash over a drawing of a generic robot. The event had happened yesterday. I shrugged it off. People would calm down in a few days, and there were other places in the market I could buy fine plantain.

It was when I was looking at the peppers. I remember because I smelled it. Sniffed it in the air. I'd sniffed and sniffed. I was looking at habanero peppers, yet I was sensing a different type of pepper over the habaneros. Something in the air was hot and charged; something was burning. I assumed it was my neural implants acting up again.

I groaned, wrinkling my nose, muttering, "Make it stop." Nothing new, though. When you made changes there were always small unexpected results along with the larger expected ones.

I'd been building on myself for years. Why shouldn't I? I've been doing it ever since I was legally old enough to make those choices. My latest augmentations were the neural implants I'd gotten six months ago. I was still getting used to them. Olaniyi hated them; he believed "enough was enough," but who was he to decide?

I'd had memory issues since I was fourteen, because of the car accident. That's nearly half my life. Long before I was a thought in Olaniyi's uncomplicated mind. My memory issues got progressively weirder as I grew older. I started seeing things happening backwards. It was horrible and jarring. Imagine trying to cross a street and just before you make a run for it, you see all the cars and trucks driving backwards exactly as they would in real chronological time. It was like being psychic backwards.

I forget what the doctors called it; there was a scientific name. They said it was attributed to feedback from artificial neural connections in my arm mingling with the natural ones in my brain and the cellular and digital connections all around me. They are still studying the phenomenon. The moments wouldn't be long, but when they happened, I always wanted to grab my head and start screaming. I refused drugs (drugs tend to cause new problems worse than the ones they fix) and no amount of therapy worked to stop it.

So I tolerated it. For *years*. Then when they reviewed my files and contacted me last year with the opportunity to get implants that boosted memory, increased my brain's mental ability, and would stop my problem, I immediately said "yes." The icing on the cake was that now I'd always be online, so there'd be no issues with upgrades, updates, or my cybernetic organs staying in sync with each other and my nervous system. My doctors also offered a much stronger connection for all this. I ok-ed it all. Olaniyi said he was fine with whatever I chose to do, but he also began to pick fights with me.

The implants made me better. Except that after I healed, the implants brought these vicious headaches and sometimes I smelled things. I'd been enduring them as the price I paid for normalcy. Since they didn't hurt anyone else and only hurt me a little, I just accepted them as part of my new being. No implant or augmentation was ever free of aches, pains, or strangeness; these were a small price to pay for the ability to move about the world on my own terms. And they were better than having to take a drug to treat problems caused by a treatment. Of course, Olaniyi wasn't interested in hearing any of this.

This day, my head ached and I smelled pepper. When I looked up, putting down the onion I was inspecting, I made eye contact with a beautiful man. He was sitting on a stool with some others. Some wore trousers and dress shirts; I recognized one of them, his name was Okenna Nwachukwu, a shop owner who'd sold my ex his car. Others wore agbada and sokoto; I did not know any of them. Dull and brilliant colors, dull and complex fabrics. All men.

Over the strong pepper scent, I could smell the scented oil the men wore. Sandalwood. These were probably men who'd lived in Abuja for a long time, maybe they'd been teens when the Red Eye began to pick up speed in the north. Their parents may have been the ones who shouted that desertification would surely stop and the dust storms would never make it farther than Jos. And maybe they'd been at Imam Shafi Abdulazeez's event yesterday.

I didn't like the way the beautiful man was looking at me. As if I weren't supposed to be there. I shivered, feeling the hairs on my neck rise, becoming too aware of my dexterous metal hand; the sophisticated hand of a robot. I knew it was one of the first things he'd looked at and noted. Wearing a glove only brought more attention to my arm. People there are too nosy and curious. The fingers could twist in all directions, as could my wrist. I could extend the arm to twice its length. I'd gotten my cybernetic smart arm and hand when I was seventeen, when my doctor said I'd finally stopped growing and could have the surgery. Before that, my very short arm stump had been fitted with an externally-powered prosthetic. Yes, my arm and its hand were extraordinary, still highly experimental, and to save my parents the cost, I'd opted out of the "humanizing exterior" that felt, smelled, even reacted like human flesh.

But people *knew* me in this market.

So why were people staring at me today? Maybe they'd been staring at me all along. All these years. Since I'd come to Abuja. Maybe I just hadn't noticed. And maybe I just hadn't noticed today that tolerance of me had reached critical mass. Or maybe that damn imam had really gotten into people's heads yesterday.

If you could, wouldn't you replace your damaged legs with cybernetic ones? Why hold on to malfunctioning or poorly formed flesh and bone because "we were born with it"? That's something said only by people who have no choice or have no actual experience with being . . . unable. What makes you *you*, really? I'm a mechanic. When something isn't working, you replace it with something better, something that *is* working.

"Stop staring at me," I muttered. My chest felt tight and I coughed. Some woman chuckled. Those men kept staring at me as they talked amongst themselves. I bought a bag of the onions and bell peppers I planned to use later in the evening despite my instincts telling me that I should leave.

The ground was pounded dirt that had been walked upon, stood upon, day in, day out. Sandals, boots, shoes, bare feet, the paws of cats and dogs, the taloned feet of vultures, the clawed feet of pigeons. It was soaked with spilled Fanta and Coca Cola. Sometimes it was turned to mud by the occasional rain. Leaves tumbled on it in the wind, trash was dropped on it, fruit was mashed into it. Motor oil, goat feces, chicken shit, semolina, garri. The dirt told everything. It was the greatest griot. It was blended with my tears, my skin cells, one of my torn off dreadlocks, the hot juice from my crushed peppers.

However, it wasn't blended with my blood. That was *their* blood. Only their blood. None of mine. And yes, my legs and arms and several of my organs may be 3rd Life, but I do still have human blood. And I have a human heart. For now.

They spoke, then they yelled at me in Hausa, Igbo, Yoruba, but mostly in English. I understood all of them. A good mechanic knows how to communicate with customers, even when she can't speak their language. Plus, YouTube had taught me how to build and take apart technology, and that includes the technology of language. Especially after I got the neural implants.

"What kind of woman are you?" the beautiful man asked me in English. He had a robust, well-groomed beard that he'd dyed reddish orange, full lips, bright sparkling light brown eyes. He was as tall as me and standing way too close. I could smell the perfumed oil he wore. Yes, sandalwood. One of my favorite scents.

I looked him in the eye. I could feel every part of my body, my pumping heart, my shaking hands. Adrenaline. I was furious. My head throbbed harder than ever. People knew me here. I took my time. I chose my words carefully. The beautiful Hausa man reminded me of my fiancé who'd asked the same question not long before he walked out the door. "What kind of woman are you?"

I said to him what I said to Olaniyi who hated all my augmentations so much yet still loved me, "I will never answer your question." My voice was cold, even hard, and it was low. And as I spoke, I looked the beautiful man dead in the eye, just as I had looked into Olaniyi's eyes.

And like Olaniyi, he slapped me in the face. But much much harder. Hard enough for my world to burst into silver, red and blue. It was as if Amadioha or Shango had slapped me. With an electrified hand. Like lightning. I was in a nightmare with my eyes open. I blinked and for a moment, I saw a million eyes, red red red eyes, a honeycomb of eyes, a pomegranate of eyes, all on me. Then all those men started beating me, and it was their wild eyes I saw between fists and feet. I don't know when they'd stood from their stools.

No one helped me.

I don't remember if anyone spoke or shouted. But I know that no one helped me. My eyes were open. I saw between the feet and legs, past the arms and I smelled the fear.

So I helped myself.

I was down, then I got up. No, I didn't *just* get up. There was a feeling in my head, a warm liquid itchy pain, like something had ruptured and was now freely bleeding at the back of my skull. But he'd slapped me in the face, why would I feel it in the back of my skull? Then there was what I could only call a . . . a difference. Something felt different. That's when I got up. I glanced at the sky, past the tops of the market booths. At the sun that shined down on me. The heat. Dry and clear, arid, Abuja was not the desert, but it wasn't far from the deserts of the north. It may sound strange, but to me, deserts were always a place of optimism and possibility, not death. I could always smell the desert in the air, more nearby than far away. I felt electrified. Solar energy is powerful.

I took on the beautiful man first. I don't believe in the traditional aesthetics of beauty. Not for me. For me, it is not in the look, it's in the function, the kinetics, the motion, the fluidity of moving in space and time. My body could never be beautiful by traditional human aesthetics.

I was born outside of beautiful, with a gnarled stump where my left arm should have been, my legs withered and misshapen. On the inside, I had intestinal malrotation and only one lung. When they'd seen the state of me on the sonogram in my mother's belly, they'd said that my mother's body would reject me and that would be that, but it didn't. I stayed. My parents and their church felt obligated to keep me. I don't think either of them will ever forgive me for not dying, nor will my father ever forgive my mother. So why revere the aesthetics of traditional beauty? It's like worshipping a god who cannot see you. It is choosing to never be celebrated. I wanted to be celebrated.

I was given an artificial 3D-printed second lung that expanded as I grew. They gave me the prosthetic arm and intestines made of genetically grown and enhanced spider silk. They gave me leg exoskeletons that allowed me to walk while using, and in spite of, my withered legs.

But that wasn't the only physical challenge the universe had in store for me. When I was fourteen, I was in a rare automated-vehicle accident, the only one of its kind. To this day, even the best engineers could not get to the bottom of what happened. My withered legs were crippled even further. I'd had to finally have them removed and get full cybernetic leg transplants. Because it took so long for my nerves to fuse with each leg, I learned what it was to sit or more often lie down for weeks at a time. I was in too much pain to be a wheelie.

When I was seventeen and able to give my consent to re-move the arm stump, over my parents' pleas to keep this with-ered useless piece of flesh and bone, the doctors gave me my cybernetic limb. When they explained the procedure and showed me the robotic arm, I asked, "Why cover it with flesh?" My par-ents couldn't afford it, I didn't need it. I am part machine. I am proud to be part machine. I was born twisted and strange by their standards. And after so much recovery, I was somehow amazing.

I smashed my machine fist into his flesh face. Why did these men think they could treat me like one of their women and suffer no consequence? Because I was polite? Because I yielded to them? Shrunk myself for them? They didn't know respect when it was given. My ex-fiancé Olaniyi was the same way.

When the beautiful man went down, the dirt of my local market place mixed with his blood. Another of the men jumped up and angrily knocked over the stool he'd been sitting on. This man's white agbada shined in the sunlight. His mouth hung open. He was shouting, a fist raised. He flew at me, and I saw a white wraith. I smelled dust and blood. I jammed the heel of my flesh hand into the underside of his chin and then crushed his ribs with a hard kick. People fled. There were five men total. Five men in agbadas and sokoto. Five men I de-stroyed. Everyone else ran, except for some teens who recorded it all on their phones.

And the market dirt mixed with more blood. They knew me there. As well as they could. Until I stepped out of line. Out of their knowledge. Now they know me there. This was my home. The woman on the far end sold palm oil pressed by her husband, a man who got angry with her if she talked to me for too long. The woman who fried the salty spiced termites always laughed when she saw my dexterous metal hands, but she never insulted me. These men were sitting and eating food that used fresh herbs and vegetables she grew in her own garden. The woman whose peppers I'd been looking at had been trained to be a barrister but gave all that up to live with her husband here in Abuja.

My market's dirt was mud with blood now, a blue Imam Shafi Abdulazeez flyer mashed into it. I stood over their bodies, the taste of metal in the back of my throat like smoke. I felt both destroyed and indestructible. My left arm. As I'd fought all those angry men, someone had smashed at my arm with a brick, just below the demarcation where flesh became metal. Now my left arm felt electrified. I briefly wondered if touching my left arm to my leg would create an electric current. Would the metal on metal kill me when the current jumped to flesh and rushed to my heart?

I turned. I ran.

CHAPTER 2

GPS

I couldn't stop looking at the sky as I drove. Occasionally, I spotted drones above, but they were all carrying delivery packages, so that was okay. None turned and followed me. The nightmare was over; at least the one at the market. I'd tripped my car offline weeks ago at the shop. Olaniyi had used the tracker on his phone to force connect to my car and monitor me during one of the few times I'd asked him to give me some space. I'd driven to a small hill not too far outside of Abuja. It was a dry hill where trees and plants refused to grow for some reason, maybe there'd been some chemical dumped there. It was my secret place to sit in the sunshine and just stop thinking. I don't know what he thought I was up to but thirty minutes after I arrived, he showed up, his nostrils flared, his eyes bulging, full of suspicion.

Though my car had 360 degrees of camera eyes, he claimed he still couldn't see my every move. He'd blurted that he'd been sure he'd find me fucking another man right there in the dirt, like some animal. His anger didn't leave him fast enough to stop the nasty ideas broiling in his mind from escaping his lips. Idiot. I was furious and though I forgave him, I still had to do something to calm my fury. Something quiet that he'd never be aware of unless he had the nerve to try and track me again. Tripping my car offline so he couldn't track me was the perfect solution. I should have understood then that things were going to go wrong between us eventually. He didn't try to track me again, though, so he never knew what I'd done. But in a matter of weeks he found another reason to leave me.

In this way, as I fled up the highway, heading north, the authorities could not immediately locate me, not through my car's cameras or satellite. My car had no digital footprint, I'd sprayed it with a transparent detection scrambling veneer and even *before* I met Olaniyi I'd tweaked my phone to stay incognito. This was illegal in the way that cracking phones to serve multiple people was illegal, you just made sure you weren't caught. And most people are too lazy to bother with such things; their privacy wasn't worth much.

So I was okay for now. Drones wouldn't find me unless they spotted me when I stepped out of my car or they flew down and caught a glimpse of me through the windshield. My only worry was that they would track me through my implants which were always online. I kissed my teeth. If they could, they would have by now.

I drove fast, but not too fast. This was difficult because I felt such a strong urge to flee where I was, who I was, why I was, when I was. If I could travel through time, I would have happily jumped into the machine and left everything I knew behind. My family, even my brother, my past, my present. Everything but my future. I glanced out the window as I drove past an opening to a street. On the corner sat a large yellow-brown monkey. I caught its eye as I passed, and we stared at each other as if we knew each other's stories. As the sun set, I spotted a ghost heading toward Lagos, an electric blue purple cloud that looked beautiful against the orange pink sky. It would probably be the last one I saw because of the direction I was going.

Then it was just more dry trees, a small market here and there, dusty parked cars and more dusty trees.

I drove.

And I drove.

The roads grew crumbly and pocked with potholes.

My car used its navigation to avoid them.

And I drove.

North.

When I stopped to buy some water or get a bite to eat or just to take a breath, I saw that beautiful man's face leering at me. Moments before he tried to smash my face in. I remembered his blood making the dirt into mud. And so I drove some more. My car was solar, but the sun was going down and I hadn't charged the battery the day before.

I saw a charging station and stopped for a travel-sized supercharge. My charging port was the magnetic kind, so I didn't have to get out of the car. The card I drew from was connected to my "walking man" account, so there was no record of transaction or, if there was, there was no specific location given. According to my phone and my account, I was in fifty different Nigerian cities all at once, none of them where I actually was.

The hours blended together. My skin grew oily and sticky with sweat and dust. I relieved myself in the bushes alongside the road, wiping with only the napkins and paper towels I accumulated when I picked up food, and this also left me feeling unclean. The terrain and the air grew drier, the roads rougher.

Night fell. I kept going. North. The night deepened. My GPS stopped working. When I'd used up all the charge my car's battery held, and there wasn't a charge-or-fill station or even human being in sight, I resigned myself to what I would do. By this time, I was in a state. I was exhausted, but images of what I'd done back in Abuja, what I'd left behind, and paranoid fantasies of what I was—all this was like a demon that had chased me into an underground cave. What was left of me was my technology. My body and my brain.

I reached a place where the road ended and the wilderness began and I got out of the car. I grabbed my small backpack with nothing but my cell phone, its solar charger, two bottles of water and the last of my shelled groundnuts. I was sweaty and stinky and wearing nothing but the clothes I'd worn when I'd killed all those men in the market. I walked into the desert. My legs were bionic, so I didn't worry about snakes or cold or the eventual heat. I didn't tire, though I was tired. And so so sad. As I walked, I cried. How far was I from . . . I didn't think about it. I'd know it if I came to it.

My left arm still tingled. I looked up at the sky and the stars were so bright that I felt as if I were bathing in their shine. I sang to myself, an old song that I used to hear my grandmother sing in English, "Five hundred twenty five thousand six hundred minutes. Five hundred twenty five thousand moments so deeeeeear." It was too dark to see much of anything, but when I came across a resting cow, I sat down and leaned against her smooth body. I snuggled my head against her warm side and the cow was fine with this despite the fact that I was part machine and she was not. Sleep descended quickly.

CHAPTER 3

Zagora

Why did I run to the desert? A desert with a disaster churning in its bowels? I could have fled in any direction. I had a wiped African e-passport on my phone. I could have crossed any continent border without anyone knowing who I was, no questions, no forms. Yet I went due north. I was broken, worse than when I was broken at the age of fourteen. Children are resilient, especially when they find a bright star to latch onto. My star back then was a podcast.

When I was fourteen and newly broken by the car accident, I realized that there are times when you either save yourself or you don't. It's *only* up to you. One does not simply have robot legs attached to the place where her legs have just been crushed off and then get up and walk off, better than new. First there is red pain. A beast with a shadow that swallowed my entire room. I don't remember that room being any color but shades of red. And for the first week, oh, I was drowning in it. Then I decided to stop drowning.

But before I discovered that podcast, I saw a ghost. The government townhouse in Lagos, which I grew up in, was built beside one of the city's ten receiving turbines. Every morning at 6 AM and every night at 11 and 3 AM, it would receive the energy payload. This was energy gathered, condensed, restructured and then wirelessly sent from the Sunflower Initiative solar farms in Morocco, Mali and Niger. These directable long-range wireless transfers of energy looked like giant delicate shadows that gently glowed their jellyfish purple blue. Most call them, "ghosts."

I'd awakened just in time to see the 3 AM ghost floating by my window. Its movement was slow but steady and focused. I gazed at it, wondering how people decades ago would have reacted to such a sight. *They probably would have thought aliens were invading,* I thought. I knew a bit about the invention of wireless energy transfer, but my curiosity sparked brighter and I decided to look up the inventor. She was now very old and her name was Zagora.

My eye landed on my phone and I knew what I had to do next. To move even the slightest bit was a horror and I may have screamed the entire time. No one was in the room with me. My phone was on the counter beside my bed. When I had it in my hands, tapping the touch screen caused fire to shoot all over my body, the motion of my fingers, wrist, the slight increase in my breathing. I was crying. But I found one. A podcast about Zagora and her great invention. It had been recorded decades ago and was easily the most iconic one. I didn't know it would be so central to my saving myself when I found it. At the time, I just needed something to listen to, something to take me out of my situation, my pain.

I saved it right on my phone, ready to play on the home screen. I played it once and it soothed me. I played it again and I felt hope; I began to imagine and wonder. The red was still there, but it became a tint. I listened to that podcast over and over, for months, for years.

During those times, I hurt so much as my nerves bonded with my new legs. Even as I healed, I endured strange random explosions of hot pain in the darkness that was my body. The hurt could be in my crushed legs or on my shoulder or in my face or in my mind. It filled the darkness like stars. But the podcast filled those stars with ghosts, possibilities. I listened to that podcast so many times that I memorized it. Sometimes I'd lie in my bed singing it like a song. I'd even hum the theme song at the beginning and end. To this day I can recite the entire thing the way some people can recite the Quran.

The podcast was called *Sahara Solaris*. It was written by a journalist who happened to meet and remember Zagora long before she became great. The podcast made the desert look like the place with all the answers.

The Africanfuturist: #8953_Sohara Solaris

Theme Music

Good morning, day, evening, to my listeners. You are listening to The Africanfuturist. Welcome to my show. How is everybody doing? I know it's been a while since my last episode, but these are strange and challenging times. I do hope that today's episode brings you hope and wonder and insight. It is a true and extraordinary story.

A travel journalist named Izzy once met the little girl named Zagora outside one of the old crumbling kasbahs in Skoura Ahl El Oust, Morocco. Izzy had been interested in the camel, not the girl. She approached the camel to get a better look and Zagora ran up to her. Apparently, going to see that camel was what a lot of tourists did, so little Zagora was ready. Before Izzy knew it, Zagora had shoved a camel woven from palm fronds into Izzy's hands and then stepped back, waiting. Izzy had to either move forward and give it back to her or pay for it. Zagora's move was brilliant in its manipulative simplicity.

Izzy had no dirham, so she made a snap judgment and gave the girl twenty Euros. She earned it. Zagora snatched the money from her lightning fast, but she had her reasons. Seconds after Zagora snatched the money, the hand of her little brother was there; he was seconds too late. Zagora ran off with the money before her brother could snatch it from her. And Izzy never saw her again. But that doesn't matter. Izzy remembered that girl and later, years later, Izzy put the story all together. This is what happened . . .

On that day outside that kasbah, Zagora was ten years old with black bushy hair and dusty gym shoes. She was short for her age. Her parents were nomads, and Zagora and her family lived in caves nearby. Her father was a Berber sheep herder, her mother an immigrant from Timbuktu, Mali, another desert region.

Zagora had grown up hearing her mother tell the story of the 52-day journey she made across the desert on foot from Timbuktu before Zagora was born and listening to her father sing old songs to the sheep as she rode along on her donkey. Oftentimes, she'd quietly sit, gaze at, and think about the Oracle Solar Complex in the distance that seemed to get bigger every year. The solar farm was as vast as a town and consisted of thousands of apartment-sized mirrors that shifted throughout the day, like the heads of sunflowers, to focus sunlight on a tower in the center. All this got Zagora interested in the sun. There was also that story her mother was always telling her about the day Zagora was born:

"I'd gone to Zagora to see my doctor, and you got impatient. We pulled over near some palm trees and you came into the world right there. You were born in the sun, but you were smart enough to keep your eyes closed."

So that's how Zagora got her name; she was named after the town she was born just outside of. Maybe seeing the sun through her newborn eyelids sparked something powerful in her.

Zagora took the money Izzy gave her and used it to buy a brand

*new receiver for the device she was tinkering with. Then she had a
grand amazing idea. But she wasn't quite ready to turn that idea into
a reality just yet. It took her six years, years of trial and error, learning from the Internet, studying, thinking, and going to school, for her
to reach that fateful night in the cave.*

*It was the hottest day of the year and sixteen-year-old Zagora was
standing in the sunshine when she realized how to realize the idea she'd
had so long ago. Her parents and two brothers were all in the cave,
sitting around the portable air conditioner. Her parents were debating
about a forthcoming World Cup game between Morocco and South
America, her youngest brother was taking a nap, and her middle
brother was doing school work. She took her bag of tools and climbed
into a small enclosure that she used as a work space. It was hot in there,
but she was used to it. The only book she had was a beaten up old copy
of* The Boy Who Harnessed the Wind. *She loved this book so much
and had since she'd started reading it repeatedly three years before.*

*When she finished creating the new transmitter that fateful day,
she positioned the receiver about a half mile away, far from the herd
of goats, donkeys sleeping beneath a make-shift tent and, of course,
her family. She didn't know it but the only creature near the receiver
was a snoozing jackrabbit. It was a good day to charge her power
source battery because the sun was full of rage, blazing hot and bright.
When she clicked the "transmit" button on her phone, no one in the
area would know that the future had just come to greet the present.
Except the jackrabbit who lazily awakened, saw the ghost-like shimmer coming toward it, and went right back to sleep, not feeling a
thing as the shimmer passed through it to reach the receiver.*

*It really was like the sun's ghost, this payload of energy that was
gathered, condensed, and restructured from the day's intense sunshine. Zagora watched it float across the rocky expanse and then,
once it got within range of the receiver, disappear. When she ran to
her receiver and took measurements of the amount of energy now in its*

battery, she threw her head back and laughed. *Exactly five megahertz! Enough to power all her family's appliances for the day. The same number that had been in the battery she'd connected to the transmitter. Not a single megahertz lost in the transfer. Success! Finally.* Zagora had just invented directable long-range wireless energy transfer. And because the power was converted from ionizing radiation to non-ionizing radiation before it passed to the receiver, it was completely safe to be around.

She named her invention, "Sahara Solaris," a name her brother suggested. Solaris *was the name of a science fiction book they'd found on the ground at the kasbah, most likely dropped by a tourist. They'd brought it home and taken turns trying to read it to practice their French. Eventually, she grew so bored and frustrated with it that she threw it out of the cave to be later chewed on by the goats. She and her brother had both laughed hard because it had been a windy day and the book had sailed farther than expected before landing right in the middle of a group of goats. "As it should," Zagora joked. She and her family lived right at the mouth of the Sahara desert and the sun was the whole purpose of the device, so the name was perfect.*

After perfecting the Sahara Solaris over the next year and with the help of her school teacher, Zagora managed to get it before the eyes of Oracle's CEO. That in itself is a long-winding story, involving several key elements:

1. *An overly ambitious and hateful uncle*
2. *Government officials hacking into her computer attempting to steal her Sahara Solaris notes*
3. *Government officials who tried to pay off her parents*
4. *Masked men who tried to kidnap Zagora*
5. *A village of nomads plus the director, actors, and staff of a sci-fi movie that was being filmed nearby all guarding Zagora and her family for three days and three nights before the fateful meeting*

Those in power came after every element of her life. The long and
the short of it was that it all required some powerful qualities to get to
this pivotal meeting. Focus, determination, audacity, and courage
were a few of them. Zagora recognized the battle when it came to her
and she knew she had to win it. And she was no fool, which was why
she arrived at that pivotal meeting with her parents, her school
teacher, and the teacher's best friend who was a lawyer well practiced
in community rights. The night before, Zagora had shown all four of
them her Sahara Solaris. And thus, when she entered that meeting in
the morning with the Oracle Complex's CEO and her advisors, she
knew exactly what to do.

She was seventeen years old. And as she stood before the board,
finally, she felt herself steady. Her heartbeat slowed. She was calm.
She knew why she was there and what she had to do. She was there
to save the world. Zagora had always had big dreams, despite her
small means. She imagined herself channeling the activist she and
her brother had watched on their phones some years ago, the girl
Greta Thunberg who had the nerve to speak with the entitlement of
the adult white men Zagora sometimes saw in the market.

Zagora spoke. First, she provided evidence that she had already
patented her invention.

"Okay, it belongs to you," one of the Oracle engineers growled.
Impatient and irritated. "Get on with it."

And she did. Zagora presented the Sahara Solaris with panache
and vigor. "Follow me," she then said. The group of officials followed
the girl outside, and there she gave a most astonishing demonstration
of what she had invented. There was silence. Then there was mur-
muring. Then there was applause. The CEO of the Oracle Complex
was speechless. She'd heard plenty from her advisors and assistant,
and general rumor and hearsay, but nothing was like seeing it in ac-
tion. How could this "beggar girl" who came from the desert caves
invent something so ingenious? Such a simple, precise, useful device.

The CEO knew she had to have this invention before this girl took and sold it elsewhere.

But Zagora wasn't done yet. "The metaphor of the mirrors has not been lost on me," she said. She'd practiced this speech many times at home. Always in Arabic, not Berber. She needed to be understood by everyone in the room. "You see the Oracle solar farm and think, 'This is our future.' It is a reflection of what we deserve, what we can be. It looks like a Star Wars kind of thing where all is clean and beautiful. It is. But there is also an ugly reality we, the people who live here, know well."

Zagora didn't say it in so many words, but she hinted at the fact that the land used for the solar plant belonged to people and that the government had applied capitalist definitions to that land in order to justify seizing it without the full permission of, and without compensating, those people. She said that those who approved the Oracle project decided that land was only valuable if it was "useful" and not valuable if it was not useful. If the land was desert, even if it was ancestral land that belonged to people, it was useless. This "useless" land was therefore subject to being put to "use," i.e., generating clean renewable energy for Morocco and beyond.

Zagora paused dramatically and then said, "I have a list of demands." Now, these demands were the idea of Zagora's team, especially the lawyer (who helped her patent the Sahara Solaris).

The following demands were included as part of that list:

1. That five local representatives join the advisors for Oracle Solar Farms and that they have voting power equal to the other advisors

2. *That the Oracle I Section of the plant be transitioned to a dry cooling system, instead of a wet cooling system*
3. *That five hundred permanent jobs be created and given only to Ouarzazate locals to manually clean the mirrors using no water*
4. *That the water needs of farmers be met before those of Oracle Solar Farms*
5. *That these same demands be met for every future Oracle plant in Africa (this part her mother told her to add)*

When she finished speaking, she sat down and she and her team waited. The CEO walked out of the room with her advisors. They made video-calls to investors. They all talked, debated, palavered, discussed, argued and eventually a decision was made. When they came back into the room, everyone slowly took their seats. Zagora and her team could barely breathe.

When the CEO spoke, what she said was shocking. Zagora sat there for several moments wondering if she had heard correctly. She had. The CEO was a smart woman and she saw the greatness of the Sahara Solaris immediately and that Zagora had protected her invention well. And that was why she had just approved every single one of Zagora's requests, deeming them reasonable and affordable once the Sahara Solaris was replicated on a large scale and put to use at all the plants. "Everything is about to change," Zagora whispered.

The rest is history, more or less. Over the years, as hoped, the success of Oracle led to more Oracles. The company created a new mega-project that expanded Oracle solar plants from Ouarzazate to Casablanca to Marrakesh to then to the countries of Algeria and Egypt. That mega-project was called, yes indeed, the Sunflower Initiative.

Automated solar-powered trucks loaded with equipment drove across these lands creating solar farms of five-mile radiuses. Across the desert, these trucks drove, stopped and dropped self-powered and programmed wi-fi enabled solar panels like large seeds. Thousands of them. These panels were high-powered mirrors that used patented Solargen technology and thus calibrated themselves. Upon command, they each awakened, dug in and positioned themselves as needed. And each farm would get its own Sahara Solaris. Soon each panel was concentrating light to its respective tower, and this energy was gathered, harvested and sent via Sahara Solaris to receiving turbines all over Morocco, Egypt and Algeria.

It was Zagora's mother (now an advisor at Ouarzazate Oracle) who encouraged Zagora to push for expansion into Mali. "The solar plants are being built in Morocco, Egypt, Algeria, predominantly Arab nations," she said. "What about Black Africa? Have those Sunflower Initiative trucks build a plant near Timbuktu? The city would finally thrive again!"

Zagora's father agreed, "If this is an African endeavor, it should be an African endeavor." And this was exactly what Zagora said at the next big Oracle meeting. On that day, the other board members dismissed her claims as unimportant. But the third time she brought this idea to the board, they listened. Zagora was the creator of the Sahara Solaris and she had earned her place at that table, she'd created that table. Plus, researchers had recently informed three of the board members that it made sense financially to expand into Mali and Niger and capitalize off of that location.

Zagora's mother helped decide the precise location for Timbuktu Oracle, negotiating with local desert tribes, tribunals, and the Mali government. The location just outside of the city of Timbuktu turned out to be a prime one because the land was flat and the sunshine was constant. Once Oracle brought renewable and free energy to the ancient city of books, sand, and mud brick, it came back to life in a way it had not for centuries. On top of this, the money that came in from exporting the energy to nearby nations was incredible.

At the same time, the Sahara landgrab (where wealthy African countries like Nigeria, South Africa, Ghana, and Egypt began buying up desert lands to build Oracle Plants that used Sahara Solarises) happened. Even the not so wealthy nations, like Mali, Chad, Somalia, and Sudan joined in the buying, albeit on a smaller scale. After African nations had their turn, China, the United States, the UK and other eager nations made deals.

Within that first decade, the African nations of the Sahara were fifty percent solar powered, the strength of the energy they produced second only to what is currently gathered from the Oracle turbines in Nigeria's Red Eye. Nevertheless, Zagora's Sahara Solaris did something that no one could have imagined. Not only did the Sunflower Initiative bring clear renewal energy to the region, but all the Oracles began to export energy to the rest of Africa and weaker payloads of it to Spain and Italy. The shimmering ghosts from energy payloads are a common sight to those who live in their paths.

The change can be seen from satellite; the continent of Africa more lit up than ever. And regardless, the always-consistent sun roils and broils 93 million miles away, offering its gifts and curses, depending on where we are, what we want and what we do with it.

Theme music

And this is The Africanfuturist. I hope you enjoyed today's episode. Aluta continua.

What a story. And even more powerful because it was true. Whenever that theme music would bubble into the narration, I'd smile. Comforted. Zagora the girl from the desert caves was optimistic and imaginative, and that gave her the ambition she would use to change the world. At the end of the podcast, there was always an ad for Zagora raffia camels like the one the young Zagora sold to the journalist. I never bought one. I was a fan, not a fool.

As I lay in that bed when I was fourteen, unable to get up yet, watching ghosts pass by my window, giving me that electrified feeling in my arm that made me feel like I could use it to do anything, I wished so hard that I could speak to Zagora. Not the beloved 84-year-old woman with millions of social network followers who still lived in those caves (though she'd built several of them into beautiful homes) that she was at the time, but the girl she'd been. The girl who loved the desert so much that she found a way to make it the most sought after place on Earth, a place of infinite potential and hope because the sun shined hardest on it. She seemed like she'd be a good friend who would understand me.

CHAPTER 4

Liquid Sword

I dreamt of the road. That it was night and I was driving and driving in a dark my headlights could barely light. And I wasn't afraid. If I drove into a car-sized pothole, so be it. If I drove over spokes set in the road by armed robbers and I was forced to stop, so be it. If I ran out of electrical charge, so be it. And if everything became dust because I'd driven so far north that I'd finally reached the beginning of Africa's greatest disaster area known as the Red Eye, so be it. For some reason, I didn't fear any drones. I just kept driving.

When I awoke, the first thing I remembered was that I had no car to drive. I stretched, feeling so rested that I wondered if I'd slept for two days. I sighed without opening my eyes, filling my lungs with fresh air. So I hadn't gone so far north that I'd entered the disaster zone. *Good*, I thought. It wasn't windy yet, but there was a strong breeze now. I flared my nostrils and inhaled it more deeply. The air flowed smoothly down my nasal cavity into my lungs. It smelled of . . . body. I frowned. And manure. Then, I caught a hint of something else. Sweet and earthen, woody. I gasped, my eyes shooting open. I sat up.

Then I froze, my mouth open. Too many things. The most immediate was that I was looking down the barrel of a gun.

The cow I'd been sleeping against slowly got up. I got up with her, keeping my eye on the man holding the gun. He was dark skinned with dark pupils, the whites of his eyes so so white. He barked something in a language I couldn't understand, and I immediately raised my hands. "Don't shoot, don't shoot!" I screeched. "I'm sorry!"

"Eh!" he gasped and I realized my sleeves had fallen back when I put my hands up. Now he was *shouting* in a language that I couldn't understand. I stared at his mouth, as if doing so would make me understand him. His teeth were white, perfect, his tongue pink as he shoved his gun at me. He stopped shouting, scrambled forward and pressed the gun to my throat, his eyes wide.

"Please," I whispered. "Don't shoot . . . was just resting." Then I shut my eyes. I'd killed all those men. There were consequences. Of course there were. Up to yesterday, I'd lived my life by the philosophy of "do no harm." Even when it came to my transplants, if flesh had to be used, I only allowed my own flesh to be cultivated and transplanted into my body, never the flesh of any other animal. Yesterday I had broken my deepest most golden rule. I waited for the end.

He was yelling again. Then he lowered his voice and was speaking. Rapidly, as if rushing to get the words out before they escaped him. I opened my eyes and we just stared at each other. I moved my eyes from his mouth to his eyes, and he stopped shoving his gun at me.

"What are you doing to my cows," he growled. He spoke English like someone who had been taught in school and enjoyed the teaching.

"Nothing," I said. "I was . . . I was just resting."

"What kind of woman are you?"

I blinked, irritation so intense flooding into me that I lost my fear for my life and resignation to my death. I dropped my hands and he flinched. Even then I wasn't bothered. I slapped his gun to the side. "Why do you all keep asking me that?" I said. I stepped back and fell over the rump of the resting cow behind me. "Ahhh!" I exclaimed, then I just lay there, as he ran around the cow and pointed his gun at me.

"You're an abomination," he growled. "Maybe that's why you are going toward one."

"*You're* an abomination!" I screamed back. I rolled to the side and couldn't hold it in anymore.

He stood there and watched me cry. Then he sat down and just kept watching. My brain was finally processing the last twenty-four hours. I saw my hand smash the beautiful man's face. I was grabbing my purse as I left my apartment for the market. I was driving in the night. The men were staring at me. I was getting into my car. Time seemed to have both stopped and was happening all at once. I wept harder, my cheek pressed to the dirt. I covered my face with my hands and the cool of my cybernetic hand in the heat of the growing day was soothing. But I couldn't fully raise my left arm.

"Are you . . . alive? Like a human being?" he whispered. He put his gun down.

I glared at him. I could move faster than him. I could have smashed his face as I'd done to three of the men at the market yesterday. His face gave me pause and I stopped crying as I studied it. He couldn't have been much older than me, if he weren't actually younger. His skin was weathered and deeply bronzed by the sun, but he didn't look like one of those northerners who needed water. There was no worry or helplessness on his face. Instead, there was a freshness to him. And he had large dark brown eyes that were wide and observant in a way that made me think of an owl. He had sharp high cheek bones

and a large scar running up the side of his left cheek. I knew
what his question meant, so I answered it. "I am alive," I said.

A bull nearby awakened and stood up, mooing loudly.
"How?" he asked.

"Science," I said.

He picked up his thick cattle-herding stick instead. I stared
hard at it. It had no glowing tip; it wasn't a Liquid Sword, the
infamous and very illegal sword-shaped Taser-like weapon
that all the herdsman-turned-terrorists carried and used to kill
people. It was just a stick. Phew. We stood eye-to-eye, we were
both tall people. I considered sending a mental signal to my
legs, making them extend so I'd be taller. "Only bad Fulani
herdsman carry Liquid Swords . . . or *guns*," I said. "Or so I've
heard."

"Times aren't what they used to be," he said. Now he picked
up his gun. He slung it over his shoulder as he added, "And I
don't carry a Liquid Sword, *those* are torture devices. But a good
Fulani stays alive. Now go away. Leave me and my cattle in
peace." He started walking away and that was when the strange
thing happened that had happened to me a few times over the
years.

Years ago, not long after I'd had my bionic legs attached, I
was sitting in my mother's yard and a swarm of dragonflies
had zoomed around me like wasps and then landed on my
arms, head, shoulders, and become still as if someone had hit
pause. I loved dragonflies and this was both a terrifying and a
delightful moment. After about a minute, they'd zipped off
and were gone.

Something similar happened again with hens last year. I'd
been walking home with two friends, and we'd cut through
someone's yard. There were five chickens there and they'd
blocked my way to the point that my friends both started

laughing. They wouldn't move, rushing at my feet every time I tried to take a step. Then they just surrounded me and stopped. My two friends got scared and ran to get help. But by the time they'd returned, the chickens had gone about their business.

And now here it was happening again. With a white cow and a bull with horns as long as and thicker than my arms, which was scarier. They both stepped in front of me. "What are you doing?" the man asked, turning around.

"I'm not doing anything!" I snapped, backing away from the large bull directly in front of me. The man started speaking in his language at the two cattle, but neither animal responded. "What is happening?" he asked.

The cattle seemed to relax, the bull mooing and the cow backing away from me a bit. But not enough where I could leave. "Fine," the man said. "You come with us."

"Huh? Where?"

"Where were you trying to go?"

I paused. Then I just grinned sheepishly at him knowing how I sounded when I spoke. "I have no idea . . . I was . . . I don't know."

He narrowed his eyes at me. "So close to the Red Eye, with no anti-aejej, nothing, and you . . ." He clucked his tongue and nodded. "Is this suicide?"

"No," I said.

"So why are you going north without any guide or supplies or plan?"

I looked away. "I don't know."

"What are you called? What's your name?" he asked.

"Unit 83204" I said.

He frowned deeply, cocking his head and stepping back from me. "You're sure you are alive?"

I raised both my hands, laughing. "I'm just joking."

"Today is a bad day to joke with me," he muttered.

"For me, today is the best day to joke," I said. "If I don't make jokes, bad things happen. My name is AO Oju."

"AayOh?"

"Like the two letters, then Oju," I said. "AO stands for Autobionic Organism. I changed my name when I was twenty years old. My parents were so angry. They prefer the name they gave me, of course, Anwuli Okwudili."

"You legally changed your name to two letters? Or you just abbreviate your real name to . . . ?"

"My name is AO," I snapped. "And it stands for Autobionic Organism." I paused, taking a breath to quell my annoyance. I hated when people questioned what I told them to call me. My name is *my* name. "What do I call you? Or shall I ask, 'What did your parents name you?'"

He paused, pursing his lips, then for the first time since I'd met him, he smiled. Then actually laughed, looking at one of his steer who looked placidly back at him. Then he looked right at me. "My name is DNA."

I blinked and then laughed so hard that I stumbled back and my left arm started twitching. "What!" I shouted and then fell into gales of laughter. What a relief it was to look up at the blue clear sky and laugh and laugh. I laughed until there were tears in my eyes. I looked into the eyes of one of the steer and laughed even harder.

"It's just my initials," he said, when I finally started calming down. He was leaning on one of his steer. "My name is Dangote Nuhu Adamu. I'm a man of tradition, a son of the sand, I'm fully human."

"Yet, you still ended up with an acronym for a name, just like me," I said.

He narrowed his eyes at me, waiting for me to say more. When I didn't, he swiftly turned and said, "Come on."

"Where?"

"Do you really care?" he said over his shoulder.

I watched him go for a few moments, until the cow came up behind me and shoved me into walking right behind DNA. The male walked beside me, its huge horns easily reaching feet higher than my head. I watched his hooves as we walked, grounding into the gravelly sand with each step. I glanced up at the clear blue sky. Not a drone in sight.

———

I'd been following the stranger who called himself DNA across the dry land for over an hour. At about the time that I finally stopped thinking over and over "What are you doing, AO? What the *fuck* are you doing??" I noticed his hands. His left hand. His right carried the stick, which he swung side to side as he walked, lost in whatever thoughts were plaguing him. I say plaguing because of what his left hand was doing. It was shaking.

"Are you all right?"

"Eh?" he said, turning around, clearly irritated by my voice. His two steer were trudging along beside us, completely uninterested in our exchange. "Your hand is shaking, *o*," I said. "Is something bothering you?"

"No." He turned around and then tripped over his feet and nearly went sprawling.

"Hey," I said rushing over.

"Don't," he nearly shouted, holding both of his hands up. He stood up and started walking. "Don't touch me!" He started speaking what I was sure was Pulaar, his people's language, and walking faster. I strode up beside him and matched his gait. For several minutes, we walked like this. Fast and silent. The steer had no problem keeping up. Ahead of us was arid land with sprays of dry bushes or palm trees here and there. It was amazing that this was still Nigeria, a Nigeria that I could drive to myself in less than 24 hours. I grew impatient.

"Hey," I said.

He kept walking.

"Hey!"

Still kept walking.

"HEY!" I shouted. Even the steer stopped. The land around us was now so vast and flat, that it seemed to swallow my voice. Not a road in sight. It was like being on another planet, no atmosphere, or so much atmosphere that everything about you is swallowed, from your sins to your voice. He stood, staring hard at me.

"I don't know you," he said.

"I don't know you, either, but I still want to know. Why are your hands shaking? Are you ill?"

He paused and then said, " No."

We stared at each other, the breeze swirling around us hot but nowhere near as hot as it could get out here, I was sure. I wiped sweat from my brow. He wasn't sweating at all. The bull sat down beside me and snorted softly.

"Why do you care?" he asked.

"Why am I out here with you in the middle of nowhere?" I said.

"We are somewhere. *You* come from nowhere."

"What happened to you, DNA?"

He started walking again, his back stiff, his gait holding that steady pace. In another hour of walking, the gravelly sand would submit to shifting sand dunes, the only voices on the

wind the occasional mutter of one of his steer. And I'd be completely alone with this man . . . and him with me. I sighed. My
left arm twitched, and the ache of it reached the flesh of my
shoulder. "Hey," I said more firmly, stopping. "What *happened*
to you? Why is there dried blood on your shirt?"

He kept going, hunched and practically stumbling forward.
"Look at you. You're not even walking properly, now."

He stopped and turned to me and the sight of his face took
my breath away. His face was wet with tears, his eyes squinted
with a pain so sharp I could have sworn I could hear it in my
ears. "What happened?" I asked yet again. DNA dropped his
herdsman's stick. And it seemed like DNA died right there on
his feet.

My father once told me about how his grandfather had
died standing. He'd gotten up that morning, kissed my grandmother, fed their dog Bingo, picked up his mobile phone, and
checked his email. He'd gone to the porch and looked out
across the city of New Calabar, and at some point he just died.
And that was how my grandmother found him. Standing and
looking at the city. However, my great grandpa died happy. In
this moment, DNA looked like the most broken man on earth.

"Ah-ah, are you going to faint?" I asked, tapping him on
the chest. He roused from wherever he'd gone. He leaned toward me and narrowed his eyes all the way to slits. I leaned
back. "What?"

"Are you a spirit?" he asked. "You must be because only a
spirit would stay around me when I am feeling like this."

"I'm not a—"

"Look at you," he said. "You're more machine than human.
It's because you are a spirit that you can animate cold metal."

"No. It's because of science," I said flatly. "And I'm actually
mostly *human*."

He kissed his teeth. "Science is mostly witchcraft," he said. "See what it has done to humanity, and the more science there is, the more there is to see. You are a spirit."

"Whatever," I sighed. "But tell me, what happened to you?" We'd started walking again, my legs taking me ever forward with this man with blood on his ankles and shirt, toward a disaster, leaving my life behind. Maybe I *was* becoming a spirit; that would explain a lot. I held my left shoulder and worked my arm. As the dry hot wind rushed past bringing up tumbling grains of sand, I could have sworn it felt better. A little. Maybe.

"Fine," he finally said. One of his steer mooed loudly. We trudged along for another minute, then he started talking. The tale DNA told was grim. And it all happened yesterday, too. As I listened I thought two things. 1. Nothing is a coincidence 2. When you decide to leave all things behind, you begin a new chapter.

CHAPTER 5

His Story

You can't understand unless you comprehend what it is to be a true Fulani herdsman. Our creator Geno first crafted stone, then stone crafted iron, then iron crafted fire, then fire crafted water, then water crafted air. When the chain reaction was complete and the Great Experiment had cooled, Geno descended again. This time, the creator took the five elements and crafted the cow, then woman, then man. From a drop of milk, Geno extracted the universe, and, now, even in the desert, the rivers of milk flow. That is our most ancient cosmogony. It's mostly forgotten, but I bring it back, I remember it and I will teach it to my future daughters and sons and they will remember it, too.

Before the Red Eye, we were almost gone. Most of us left the lifestyle or were killed off. First the desert swallowed the lands we'd roamed for centuries. What used to offer our steer plenty of food, became barren packed dirt, stone, and sand. We moved south and many of us, disenchanted and enraged by loss, began to violently clash with farming communities. Most of us even let our steer go and took up arms and fought and took from the farmers. They killed us, we killed them. The government tried to force us to settle, but nomads will always be nomads and thieves will always thieve. Plus, farmers will never share land. That is not their nature. So the killing started again. The farmers won, nearly wiping us out.

Then the Red Eye came. You have to understand, AO. The

disaster saved us. Years ago, when the Red Eye was born and began to spin, the farming communities who lived on the border fled their villages and towns. These were thriving communities of just about every ethnic group in the country. Their farms had irrigation systems. Capture stations cemented into the ground provided all the water the farm needed. These people were terrified by the Red Eye. It is understandable if you have seen it. The sight of it, looming. Yes, it is understandable. They left, but they could not bring their cemented irrigation systems, so those stayed. And continued watering the abandoned farmland.

Over the years, those lands continued growing, spreading, grasses joined the crops that kept coming back. And herdsmen had places to graze their cattle away from people. When I set out with my steer, I was only fifteen and those lands were their buffet. Still are. There are more of us but still so few of us. The beef we provide is the finest.

The cattle of the Fulani herdsman represents and holds the heart of the community, even those who have forsaken the traditional life. They are our relatives, my brothers and sisters. We name them, we care for them, we respect them, we love them. You can't understand it because you are not one of us, we are few now, only a few hundred live my culture, but you must understand these things to understand what I am about to tell you. To . . . to understand me.

We shouldn't have passed through that the town of Matazu yesterday. The warning was nothing definite or true. It was . . . a smell. The place didn't smell right. We understand how things have happened in the past. So usually we leave our cattle outside town with a few of us guarding them when we go in to buy supplies, but times have gotten strange, and dangerous. So we brought them with. We brought a parade *of steer, yes. Maybe 100, all together. This farming community didn't like it, but we were only passing through. All we wanted were some bottles of soda and water, cooking oil, sacks of groundnuts and dates, new toothbrushes, things. And we did not allow our cattle near any of their farms.*

After my father died, my mother joined one of the female-led nomad groups living in the far north, and that's where she had me, months later. She taught me that wherever we went, to always take two minutes to stop and feel a place. My mother hated wearing shoes, so, to her, this meant placing her feet firmly on the ground of wherever she was, closing her eyes and letting her being spread around the place like dust. Imagine every breathing thing, human, cattle, insect, plant, pulled into you, floating into every crevice, over every surface and then taking a general pulse, temperature, blood pressure. She said to do this even when you only planned to be in a place for a minute.

It's the deepest Nomad Code. So deep that most nomads have forgotten it. It makes you a part of wherever you go, so you are never alone, you always have a place. I still do that to this day. I did it to this town and that's what saved my life. I'd stopped just at the place where the small town began, my cattle around me. The others went into the town ahead of me. Ibrahim and Aminu were both annoyed with me for taking so long. They too had a bad feeling about this place and wanted to get in and out quickly.

We don't always pay attention to the news. We shut our phones off. Especially when we are with our cattle and on the move. You have to watch your people when you move. You have to use all your eyes. We'd met up two days earlier. We herdsman go it alone except for a few days every three months where we meet with our closest comrades and catch up. My comrades Aminu and Ibrahim had wives, so they were with us, too. Ibrahim has two children, but both happened to be with their grandparents . . . and that was good on this day. We were all so happy to sit and catch up that we didn't check our phones or windows. We'd been on the move since before sun-up. And so we hadn't heard about the incident at the church in this town two days ago. Four armed men calling themselves "herdsmen" had set upon a church and shot six people before making off with cell phones, tablets, windows, and passwords.

They were dressed *like herdsmen, but witnesses said they'd arrived in the town by bus. Where were their cattle? If I had to guess, I'd say they were probably men hired by the Ultimate Corporation to cause problems with farmers, to smear the herdsman reputation. They had charged up Liquid Swords and they used them to electrocute and slice up seven people, five of those people died. This was the town we strolled into with our 100 cattle, ignorant of what had transpired so recently.*

It didn't take long, AO. It didn't take more than a few minutes. I saw it about to happen right before my eyes. Up the road, just where the town began. As I stood and took my moment, trying to pull in and take the pulse of my surroundings, as my mother had taught me, I smelled it first. It smelled alkali and mildewy. Old for its age. Sad.

I watched them surround Ibrahim and hack him to death and then his wife as she tried to run away. Others began hacking at his cattle. It was horrific, the precision. They knew exactly where to cut to take down a steer in one chop. They worked so fast. As if they had trained for this! Then they took Aminu. His wife only stood there in shock. She didn't try to run. She was the one with two children and she didn't try to run. Then Aminu's cattle and mine, too. The whole street began to smell like blood. I don't know why, but I just stood there as Aminu had. Yet no one noticed me. I was still in my moment, I pulled the town into me, I'd settled on its surfaces, into its crevices. Maybe that's why it took so long for anyone to see me or my cattle.

I heard a steer near me bellow. A guttural sound. It had already been chopped down. Those were death cries. Star. She was falling in pain and a woman standing over her had a machete raised. She was going to chop at Star again. This was when I finally raised the gun I'd always kept slung over my shoulder, and I fired. I did this before I even knew I did and the woman twitched and stumbled back, Star still braying in pain. There was a mist of blood from where the bullets hit the woman. I felt it spray over me. Now the air smelled of her blood, Star's blood, so much blood. It wasn't the first time I'd had to kill, and I still screamed.

More chopping sounds and then bang and bang, again. They were shooting some of the steer in the head. Executions. More towns-people had come to kill the rest of my cattle. For some reason, no one came for me as they did my friends. There were people from that town all around me. Mouths open, machetes raised, guns up, shoot-ing, hacking, blood and flesh in their eyes, on their hands, spattering their feet, flying in the air. But no one saw me. Even after I'd shot the woman.

At some point, I turned and called my cattle and those of us who could, ran. Only two of my thirty cattle made it out of that town with me. Two! They killed the rest, along with my comrades. The road was dirt, despite all the brick and mortar buildings and autonomous vehi-cles made for the paved road. This served us well, because when we ran, we kicked up clouds of dust, making it harder for them to follow. I jumped on my cow Carpe Diem and rode her and that was how the three of us escaped.

When we reached a place over a hill that led into the desert, we stopped. I brought out my phone. I saw the news. They were calling my friends and me "herdsman terrorists" and said we'd returned there to attack the town yet again and instead gotten attacked. It reported the "victory" as a blow against herdsman violence after a great tragedy. I saw one photo before I shut my phone. It showed the *townspeople celebrating, as if they'd won a war. People in the photo were roasting the meat of the cattle they'd killed over open fires. Some of those had to have been mine. Had they even removed the bodies of my friends? Or did they roast and eat them, too, in their violent fog?*

And now, here you come into my troubled life.

CHAPTER 6

Sense of Wander

So I'd killed yesterday and so had DNA. And he'd nearly been killed and watched his friends and "family" killed. What kind of strange coincidence was this? I massaged my glitching arm, blinking. Throughout his telling, not once had I thought about my own yesterday. How could I? I stared at him. "I'm sorry," I whispered.

"This blood," he said pulling his shirt. "It is not mine. It is that woman's. The woman I shot. Killed." He rubbed his face with one of his large calloused hands and looked off toward the open land. He looked back at me, and I flinched. There were more tears in his eyes. "If you are truly sorry you will tell me why you are out here."

I pressed my lips together. "You don't want to hear it." I almost said that it didn't matter.

"Tell me, if only to help me get my mind off what I lost last night."

"Filling your mind with more loss to fill a void of loss isn't—"

"Please," he said. "Oh *please*, just tell me." More tears fell from his eyes. "Please. Or I will break." He shivered. "I am dead. I want to die." He grasped his head, sitting right there in the sand. "I want to die, AO. They're all dead."

I looked down at him, rubbing my sore and glitching arm. I still couldn't bring forth the words to recount what I'd done yesterday. "You won't die," I said. "You . . ." But I quickly shut my mouth. He'd lost dear friends. And to tell a herdsman who has just lost most of his herd that he could always buy more cattle was as callous as telling a mother who'd lost a child that she could always birth more children.

"Tell me what happened," he begged, still holding his head in his hands.

The weight of it all settled on my shoulders, or maybe it had always been there. I felt so so heavy. I sighed and looked at the sky and then I looked at him. "Okay. But put your gun over there." Without hesitation, he brought the strap of his gun over his head, walked to his only remaining bull and dropped his gun beside the sitting animal. He came back to me and stood waiting, his arms across his chest. I had nothing left to lose. I took a deep breath and sat down. When he too was sitting, I told him.

But I was wrong; I *did* have more to lose. I had a big imagination. I had a powerful memory and it was bolstered by neural implants. I had a keen eye for detail. And I may have been fifty percent machine, but I had the emotional range of a healthy empathetic human being. And so recounting all that led me to that moment in the desert crushed me again.

———

"And now, here I am."

I shut up and waited. He would get up and flee any moment and I'd be out in the desert all alone. I was already ahead of him; I knew what I'd do. I'd watch him leave and then keep walking until I became a ghost. Or robot. Wasn't that why I came out here? I massaged my temples hard, the headache inside pounding from a deep place. A strong breeze blew, coating both of us with sand. Neither of us moved.

"Are you having the headache now?" he asked, looking closely at me.

"Yes," I snapped. "Yes. And if you're going to leave me, just leave me. No more talking." Now I was the one tearing up. It was like the electrical current that ran within my legs and arms had jumped rails and decided to use the fluids in my brain like circuitry. Circuitry that operated to the beat of a drum, *thoom, thoom, thoom*. The pain flared and the breeze blew more stinging sand on us. I was sad, so deeply sad. I was still alive, but everything just felt . . . over. Nothing left to do but reach the end and fall over the edge once and for all. *Oh my God, is this all there is?*

DNA muttered something, but it was in Pulaar so I didn't know what it was.

"Whatever makes you happy," I said, straining against the pain in my head. "Whatever you want. Whatever you all want."

He kept muttering. The only word I caught was "Allah." He was praying. Or maybe he was cursing. I didn't care. He stood and held a hand out to me. His eyes were red and there was a large crusted narrow scratch near his right wrist. "Get up."

"No," I said.

Surprisingly, he smiled. But it was a sad smile. "Neither of us will die here. Not yet." He knelt down and took my left hand. He hesitated for a moment, looking at my steel fingers. He grasped more firmly and pulled. I let my weight keep me on the ground. He stepped back. "They'll all be after you. Even if you have no identity. They *still* have satellite. The good thing is they see this place as dead, though I hear that sometimes they'll even follow you into the Red Eye if they want you badly enough."

"Yeah. They'll find me eventually," I said. "I'm doomed."

"Then maybe we stop talking and get moving."

"To where?"

"My village," he said, bringing a dusty battered phone from his pocket. "They're true nomads, so they move around. Not even Ultimate Corps can track a nomad village, let alone the government. Right now, my village should be relatively close."

"But I thought Fulani herders had no, uh, village."

He kissed his teeth and shook his head. "More misinformation. Villages can move around and many of us haven't been nomads for over a century."

"So how do you find your, uh, village?" I asked.

"There's a code. I can find them, but the government never can."

Nomads who could not be located by anyone but tribe members. I'd thought I was ahead of everyone by hacking my identity offline, yet here was one of the oldest cultures in West Africa ahead of everyone because they wanted to hold on to a key part of their traditional way of life. Using the new tech to maintain old ways.

I let DNA pull me up.

━━━━━

I walked with my eyes on my sandals. Crunching down on the rough sand and hard pebbles. The sun was beating my shoulders, its heat passing through my veil and the material of my dress. My arms and legs remained cool, the metal they were made from didn't heat in the sun. I chuckled to myself and DNA glanced back at me.

"Are you all right?"

"Are you?" I asked.

He turned back around without a word, his arms rested on the stick over his shoulders. Behind me trudged his two remaining cattle. The bull's name was "GPS" because he never wandered off. The cow's name was "Carpe Diem" because she had a habit of getting up before all the other steer in the morning. Back when he had other steer.

He started singing. A popular ballad by a rock band that I was always hearing streamed while I worked in the auto shop. It was one of those songs that stole heavily from children's nursery rhymes, using a lot of repetition and sing-song language set against an acoustic guitar. It was actually a beautiful song despite its mainstream appeal, and now DNA belted it out over the dry land. I raised my head, the smile on my lips surprising me. I joined in.

Neither of us could sing all that well, so I'm sure the steer were glad when the breeze carried our voices into the distance ahead of us. Singing always raised my spirits; it was no different now. DNA seemed the same. The worry and shock in his face were gone. The breeze blew dust at our backs and we sang into it as if we were singing into futures.

CHAPTER 7

Gold

The man, the cat and the dog came over a sand dune like magic. One minute we saw nothing but sand, the next there was a man at the dune's peak, and he was waving at us. "Saw you all from a mile away," he said from the top of the dune. "Plus, you four make a ton of noise out here, even with the wind." He was a small compact man of about forty with a head full of tight, short salt and pepper dreadlocks and a mouth full of gold teeth. At his feet were a hearty tabby cat and an equally hearty pointy-eared blue-gray dog with bright blue eyes. They trotted to GPS and Carpe Diem.

"What is that?" I asked, pointing behind the man.

It looked like a rusted, bicycle-sized white box resting on two fat wheels. The top and sides of it were green with leafy hanging plants. As it slowly, steadily scaled the sand dune, heading right toward us, a narrow white funnel shot up from it, reaching high into the sky. It made a loud *whoooooosh!* and the air around us grew comfortably cool. The contraption had a capture station collecting water. I laughed. This was why the green plants on it stayed healthy; they had an easy, constant source of water.

"That's a planter, isn't it?" DNA asked, grinning.

I looked around. Planters were the property of Ultimate Corp, and Ultimate Corp always monitored its equipment.

"Relax," the man said. "They actually *don't* monitor planters. That's how rich Ultimate Corp is. They hire us. They pay us
if we send invoices. They record how many plants we plant.
And they're so confident in our desperation and so rich that
they don't bother checking on us if we go rogue, as I have."

"You don't plant?" DNA asked.

"Oh I did for a year or two, then I decided it was time to go.
I know you think I'm touched, but I don't need money."

DNA shook his head. "I don't think you're, uh, touched.
Out here, money isn't everything."

The man nodded. He squinted at the cat rubbing itself
against his legs. Then he looked at us and held out a hand to
DNA, "I'm Gold. Who are you?"

DNA looked at me, and I shrugged. He took the man's
hand and shook it. "DNA."

I held out my left hand and he took it without hesitation
and shook it firmly. "Ah, you must have walked away from Ultimate Corp, too," he said to me, smiling.

I frowned. "Why do you say that?"

He motioned toward me. "Because you're part made from
their stock, and you're out here."

"I'm not part . . . I was born . . ." I frowned and shook my
head. "I'm not a . . . a product of Ultimate Corp."

He chuckled. "Suit yourself," he said patting me on the
shoulder. "I didn't mean to offend, my dear. I think you're
amazing." He looked beyond me. "Pepper has made friends
with your steer."

I looked back, then I laughed loudly. The dog stood on
Carpe Diem's back and the steer didn't seem to mind at all.
DNA, however, looked irritated. "Don't worry," Gold said.
"Relax. We are all happy and healthy." He put two fingers in his

mouth and blew a brief sharp whistle. The dog leaped down
and came running. "He was raised around cattle," Gold said.
"He's used to herding them."

"Well, my steer aren't inanimate objects," DNA snapped.

"They didn't mind, though," Gold said. "Pepper knows
how to tread lightly. Anyway, come, let's break bread. I have
fresh roasted goat meat and fried plantain and I'm happy to
share." He also had a giant red tent he could pitch in seconds
that provided us with solid shade and a solar fan. The whole
set-up was comfortable and the food he shared was delicious. I
hadn't eaten since the peanuts I'd had yesterday, and with each
bite, I felt more like myself. I was about to take a third helping
of the goat meat. Instead, I hesitated.

"Eat, eat," he said. "I'm coming from my sister's wedding
two nights ago. They packed my planter's cabinet with too
much food. Even with the cold of the capture station, it's so
much food that it'll spoil before I can finish it all."

I took another piece of goat meat. "Have you always traveled alone?" I asked.

"No," he said. "My best friend, she used to travel with me.
Then she decided she wanted to settle down and start a farm."
He paused and looked at the content cat sleeping in his lap.
"That was when I decided to stop planting for Ultimate Corp."

DNA laughed and nodded.

"What? I don't get it," I said.

"This your friend is not from around here," Gold said to
DNA.

"No," DNA said. "And she hasn't been here for more than
twenty four hours."

"Miss AO, you will think I'm touched and that is okay. I
still explain am to you. You go listen?"

I rolled my eyes at his dramatics. "I go listen," I said.

"Okay. Miss AO, I'm out here because I have to bear witness to what used to be here. My lady didn't want to, but that's above me now. I know I must. I was out here *before* Ultimate Corp ran everything and everyone out into the desert and into the Red Eye. Then they hired many of us nomads to leave our way of life to earn a salary by planting. We were fools.

"We let them convince us that we had nothing and our lands were useless. If it cannot make money, then it is worthless. That is not our culture, that is capitalism. Yet we still listened. We saw their big cities, we wanted all their nonsense things, we respected their big talk. We learned to prize money over things far more valuable.

"This led to farmers' letting Ultimate Corp buy their land. They were convinced they were getting something for nothing, the nothing being the land they'd been told was worthless. There was an element of fear, too. Fear of the big people from big far-away places. Goddamn, it was like rolling over and dying. The farmers sold their land, but they stayed to farm it. Where else were they going to go? They were given high tech equipment for farming which made them abandon their old ways. How can you go back to the labor of working the land when now you simply had to press buttons to make the machines do it? Now Ultimate Corp really has them. It's a mess. My friend, she married one of those farmers. At least with me, she was free."

He threw his piece of goat meat to his dog who sniffed at it and then slowly began to eat it. Pepper was a well fed dog.

"Everyone who works for it, hates it," DNA said.

Gold nodded. "But they collect a salary from it. They shop from it. They hate what it does, yet Ultimate Corp continues doing it. It's something more than human, by Allah. It's the beast, a djinn. Fire and air, insubstantial, but very real. Human beings created it, but they will never control it."

We were all quiet after that, except for the sound of Pepper politely gnawing on his piece of goat meat, the cat curled nearby in a most peaceful nap.

━━━━━

Hours after Gold had moved on and we'd walked goodness knew how many more miles, I was still thinking about all he'd said. *He took one look at me and thought I was an actual* product *of Ultimate Corp. I mean, maybe my parts came through them*, I thought. *But everything came through them.* I stopped walking. Did everything come through Ultimate Corp? "Maybe," I muttered, pinching my chin. I'd never really thought much of it.

"What?" DNA asked.

"Nothing," I said, starting to walk again.

I was sweating and looking at my feet. The networks of fine metal filaments woven around the heavier central structure gave my joints a flexibility that even made walking in sand easy. And the sand would sift right through. When I walked in mud, because of a special polymer sealant, the mud would slide right off. My feet couldn't slip on ice, get stuck in muck, stay wet, and I could walk over hot lava and the metal wouldn't melt. The joints were silent as the wings of an owl. I could jump fifteen feet in the air and land like a ballet dancer. My feet could grip even the tiniest crevice, so I could climb as well as a mountain goat.

So though my legs looked like the skeleton of a half made robot, I was marvelous. *Doesn't matter if my parts came from Ultimate Corp*, I thought. I kicked a small mound of sand. When I first got my legs and was recovered enough to actually try them out, I'd crumbled to the ground, and it took three nurses to get me back into the hospital bed. I was closely monitored for weeks because my legs could have set me on fire during the nerve regeneration and fuse phase. All it would have taken was one misfire. It was one of the reasons so few of the disabled opted for even one cybernetic leg transplant, let alone two.

There was a reason I was such an angry child at fifteen. Not only was I full of hormones, ambition, curiosity and zeal, but for most of my fourteenth year of life, my nerves were also almost constantly on fire, and it was because of some freak car accident. That year was like a rebirth. The old me died when my legs were crushed and a new me was slowly reborn.

At first, the hospital bed swallowed me, I was so skinny. With each day, I disappeared more. And I wanted to disappear. Just fade away into the sunshine. Because I was sure that something clearly didn't want me on this Earth. It had made a mistake in bringing me here, and it was doing everything it could to right its wrong.

My bed was beside the window, and my parents made sure that I was in the sunlight every day, the AC in the room keeping me cool and comfortable. I'd sit there, my pain numbed, flattened, and made strange by drugs, and stare at the dust floating about in the sunbeam shining on me. I wished I were one of those specks of dust. Insignificant, clean, free. However, as time progressed, it was as if I passed through a wall of fire. I told my doctors to take me off the drugs. My parents didn't even realize it because I told them nothing about it, and I seemed quite normal. Better than normal. I was making progress.

I began standing up on my new legs, to my physical therapist's delight. Then I was taking steps. Then I was walking around the hospital. My physical therapist couldn't wait to tell my parents how I'd walked all the way to the end of the parking lot on the gravelly median between the cars. Uneven surfaces were the toughest. All this I did while enduring pain so intense that it was like existing close to a white hot sun.

There was no way to adjust to my cybernetic legs without enduring the pain as the nerves regenerated. That's how I became so adept with my legs and later my arm. My doctor verified this for me. She said that it's something they don't like to tell transplant patients like myself, that in order to truly master usage, you had to die another death by pain. This is why most with cybernetic parts can move better than any organic human but few truly master the technology's potential. What doctor would tell their patient that they have to endure pain three times worse than childbirth, a pain that lasts for over half a year?

By the time I was sixteen, I understood so much about myself and the darkness that life can bring. I wanted to dwell in the light. Not as a speck of dust, but as a raging teen interested in touching everything. And I never forgot the pain of that awful year of life.

A flare of a headache hit me so hard that I stumbled and screamed. "Ah, here it is again," I groaned, grabbing my head. DNA rushed to me and when I looked at him, it was as if I were looking through a cascade of blood. Everything was tinted red and pulsing like my heart's beat. And I was smelling it, too. Coppery and sweet. *Am I bleeding?*

"AO, what's wrong?"

"I don't know! My head . . ." I opened my mouth and took in as much air as I could. It tasted of blood.

"We're close to my village. About a mile," he said. "Can you make it?"

I was sinking. Into the ground and into my head. I was only half aware of him helping me climb onto Carpe Diem. The breeze. Carpe Diem's momentum. DNA jogging in front of us, I felt like I'd descended further into wilderness.

Up ahead, all I glimpsed through the red haze was more desert. If his nomadic village were nearby, it must have been very very small. I'd been looking ahead into the distance, beyond DNA when it happened. Now everything was going dark and quiet and calm.

————

I heard myself exhale, then the red veil lifted. And the headache… no, the headache didn't stop exactly. There was a rupture in my head and it was followed by a feeling of liquidy warmth. An almost sweet sting. Then a looseness. Gradually, I felt better. I twisted around and rested my chin on Carpe Diem's furry head. "Oh," I whispered, looking ahead, past DNA walking with GPS. "How did I not see that?"

CHAPTER 8

Village

The nomad village was about a mile in diameter. Low Bedouin style goat skin tents set up not too close but not too far. It was nearly upon us now. A minute ago, when I'd looked up, I hadn't seen a thing. "Oh good," he said. "You look a lot better."

"Yeah," I said, sitting up. "I don't know what the hell that was."

We started encountering DNA's people and, from the start, it was strange. But before I get to that, let me note how these people lived. I'm used to concrete towers and sprawling buildings. Of course, much of Abuja, parts of Lagos and all of New Calabar are green with government-maintained swaths of peri grass. Most of the lower half of Nigeria is green with it to some extent. And drones and AI-run robots peopled the streets and the air like insects and birds. Their cooling fans are fluffy with dust and dirt, some are missing parts because people pull them off to sell in the black market.

Though I hadn't lived in wealth, I've always lived in relative comfort. Both my parents were gifted and ambitious engineers who were most interested in creating innovations for Nigeria and least interested in participating in strikes or protests. My parents were the two engineers behind the solar roadways and parking lots that powered so much of Imo State.

I'd been a baby at the time, but I still vaguely remembered the smell of asphalt and the adhesive used to seal in the solar panels. My parents were well known back home, though not all that well paid. And the government townhouse I grew up in was a solid strong structure as were all the apartments I've lived in since I moved out of my parents' home. I was a typical southerner.

So seeing how these people lived was *jarring*. Up until yesterday, I'd never spent a night under the stars, these people *lived* beneath the stars. They set up tents made from thin but colorful Ankara cloth. They were protection from the winds, not the rain. It barely rained here, apparently.

And there was one huge conical thatch structure in the center of it all. It was this that I set my eyes on because everything else around me was too much. I'm used to being stared at, but not by an entire village. Not all at once. Some wore the traditional long flowing garments, but most wore sun gear, a stylish Ankara clothing made to absorb energy from the sun into a small battery in the side pocket that could be used to power appliances. The women tended to wear sun gear with a blue or black thin veil covering their heads that went all the way down to their ankles. And they spoke English, at least around DNA and me.

"Hello, ma'am," one woman said to me. "You can't walk?" I was still sitting on Carpe Diem.

"I can walk," I said, quickly scrambling off the cow.

"It's DNA," someone said.

"Oh my goodness."

But most of the villagers just stared at us. Especially at me. They crowded around us and I immediately wanted to escape. I narrowed my eyes and squeezed my fingers into fists. I wasn't afraid of these people, but I was still jumpy from yesterday, when I was surrounded by seemingly nice people who'd then hardened into cruelty.

"Everyone move back," DNA said. "Farah, Jojo, Moham- med, everyone, it's me. What is all this?"

I noticed her first because she looked just like DNA except with braids and darker skin. Same deeply Fulani face that peace- fully blended remote Arab features and powerful West African ones. And she had the same tall lean frame. She was pushing through the people, an intense frown on her face. "Brother, come on!" she grunted as she shoved two men aside. She wore a long red abaya and a sheer red veil, and she somehow managed not to get it caught on any of those around her. She grabbed his hand and yanked him between two women.

"You people, move," she snapped. "Always sniffing for gos- sip. Go to the city if you're so bored."

"AO," DNA said, looking back at me as his sister spirited him away. "Come."

We followed her into a series of tents with entrances facing each other, not far from the large thatch structure in the center of the nomad village. These tents were all made of the same deep red cloth, setting it apart from the patchwork of tents around it. DNA's people had money.

"Go in, go in," his sister insisted, shoving DNA into an en- trance covered by two hanging red cloths.

"Wuro, stop pushing me. I'm coming," DNA snapped.

"Gololo! Mama!" she yelled.

I followed them both in, glancing behind me. Several vil- lagers had followed us, but stopped some yards away, talking amongst themselves. Then I was inside a courtyard in the cen- ter of tents lit by sunshine streaming in from above and scented with an incense so strong, no fly would dare try to endure it. Red cloth walls, flimsy yet protective, floors red with thick carpet, red leather travel bags, even the woman staring at DNA as she emerged carrying a large platter of flat bread wore red pants and an embroidered red kaftan. Red, red, red.

It happened to both DNA and me at the same time. We had just met and something had bonded us. Yes, it was mostly the traumas we'd both endured but also something else. Whatever it was, the bond was so true that we both expressed PTSD in the same way, at the same time.

We stopped where we were. DNA stood in the center of the courtyard, facing his staring mother. I was directly behind him, my face inches from the gun on his back. I was looking over his shoulder, seeing only the red cloth of the tent. Only the red.

. . . I was falling into red.

. . . Falling and flailing through time.

. . . Flailing backwards twenty four hours.

Time dumped me at the moment where men's blood was spilling a stark red onto the dirt of my market's dirt ground. Reflecting in the rays of sunshine that fought their way through the market booths and stunned hardened people. They were like stone, unmoving and unfeeling as they watched and did not help. The blood on my dexterous robotic hands, my robotic feet. I heard a whimper escape my throat, and I heard a man's throat crushed by my hands.

"Mama! Look!" Wuro said, rushing to a tall woman in red pants and a red shirt putting a tray of bread right there on the floor. DNA's mother strode to him, her hands outstretched.

"Dangote, what are you *doing* here?"

"All dead," I heard him whisper. His back was to me, but I

heard him as clearly as if I were hearing my own thoughts. I reached forward and took his hand. He grasped mine. I caught Wuro's eye as I did this, and her eyebrows rose.

"Mama," he said. "C-can't I come home? To rest? If you're worried about her . . ." he motioned to me. "She's off the grid, like us. They won't find her anytime soon."

"I don't know who this woman is," she snapped waving a dismissive hand at me. "You reject every woman we found for you. Too old, too young, too much school, too much city life. You finally bring one home and she's mostly machine." She loudly kissed her teeth.

Wuro laughed loudly.

"Mama, she's—"

"Dangote!" A man who also looked like DNA but older burst into the courtyard from another tent entrance. "Hey! He is really here!"

"Gololo, I can explain," DNA said.

"Just tell me. Is it true?" Gololo asked.

Wuro stood beside him, her arms across her chest. She shook her head, rolling her eyes. "One-track minded. Our brother is home, Gololo. Take a breath and see that for a moment."

"Is it true?" Gololo demanded.

"Is what true?" DNA asked. He looked back at me. We were still holding hands. His flesh to my steel. His eyes, still clouded with the pain of his trauma, asked me, *Do I tell them?* I looked away.

"I'm not asking about *her*," his brother snapped, pointing at me. "I'm asking about *you*. Is it true about *you*? Have you really become a terrorist?"

Wuro picked up the tray of bread, clearly anticipating trouble. She ducked out of the tent, and I wished I could do the same.

"Terrorist? Me?? Why would I . . . ?"

His brother stepped closer. "If the stories aren't true, where are your steer? Just GPS and Carpe Diem? Where is everyone else? Why come home without them? What herdsman would *do* that?"

"I came home *because* . . . wait, what stories?"

His mother grabbed his shoulder and thrust a phone in DNA's face. And in that way, DNA saw himself shooting the woman yesterday. He must have felt as if he'd suddenly time-travelled backwards and landed just outside of his body. I was standing right behind him, so I could see the footage clearly. The point of view was from in front of DNA and close enough to catch the twitchy look on DNA's face just before he blew the woman away.

The bullet hit the woman in the chest and there was a mist of blood. Then the woman fell. As DNA stared at the footage, his back was to me, so I couldn't see his face. But I saw his head twitch, and I heard him whimper. He grabbed his head and started screaming like a mad man. Right there in the middle of his family's nomadic compound, villagers outside eavesdropping, the sun shining down on us all.

Wuro burst back in and tried to grab him, but DNA jerked back, inconsolable. His mother stood there, her eyes wide with shock, still holding up the damn phone. His brother was beside her, mouth agape. "What's wrong with him?" Wuro screeched, reaching out, tears in her eyes. I snatched the phone from his mother's hand and threw it down. I heard a satisfying crack. "What the hell are you *doing*? You think he needs to *see* that?"

His mother didn't miss a beat. Her youngest son was still screaming as she pointed a finger in his face. "My own SON! Terrorist! Terrorist! Killing people like they are lizard! Shame!"

Her finger was practically in his open mouth and I wondered if, in his hysterics, he'd bite it off.

DNA had stopped screaming and now just stood there, a blank look on his face. I've seen people in this state before. They're wound as tightly as they can wind. If you touch them, if you even try to speak to them, they explode. Like my mother when she learned her father had died. I'd been five years old and sitting in the auto chair I liked to use when the exoskeletons on my withered legs made me tired. I was right beside my mother when her phone buzzed. She had spoken to her mother using the speaker, so I'd heard the entire very brief conversation. Her father had died peacefully in his sleep while sitting in his favorite chair, and her mother had found him.

I stared at my mother as she whispered, "I'm coming, mama. Right away." Then she'd put the phone down and gone quiet and still. When minutes had passed and she was still frozen and staring off into space, I touched her shoulder ever so lightly with my right hand and whispered, "Mama, are you all right?"

My mother erupted into screams, tears, motion. Slapping and punching the air. My chair sensed the danger and it immediately zipped me across the room to safety, where I watched my mother lose her shit for the first and only time in my life.

DNA was like this now. And this time, I knew to move myself away.

"Why?" his brother asked. "Why would you give up your cattle to become *trash*?"

This seemed to snap DNA out of it. The word "trash" or maybe it was the sharp way his brother said it. Like a machete. DNA blinked and then grabbed his brother by the collar and started shaking him like a ragdoll. "I am NO TERRORIST!" He looked his brother squarely in the face. He shook him some more. "You believe what you see on the screen posted by people you've never met over your own heart? You *know* me, brother. I WOULD NEVER."

"I know what I *saw with my EYES*," his brother said, tearing himself from DNA's grasp. "The whole thing was recorded. I saw it live."

DNA laughed ruefully. "You yourself told me that footage can be manipulated! Anything digital!"

"That was the first thing I checked for!" he snapped. "I know the digital fingerprints of manipulations. That's not hard to detect with the right tools. Which. I. Have. What I saw had NOT been manipulated."

"Did you see the *whole* thing?! *All* the footage? What kind of journalist isn't interested in *context*?" He turned to the crowd that had gathered inside at all four entrances. DNA squared his shoulders, and I stepped to the center of the space, looking around, unsure of what he was about to do. More people were coming in, joined by his mother who'd picked up her cracked phone. She stood behind DNA's brother.

"I just wanted to be left alone," DNA said, looking defiantly at me. He turned slowly, addressing everyone around him. "You *all* know me. Everyone here knows the business of everyone here. We're family. I didn't want to leave for the cities, I didn't want school, I wanted what our earliest forefathers wanted: A wife who was simple like me, children who'd do whatever children did and my cattle. THAT IS ALL. I don't want big money, big houses, big land, big items. I wanted to grow up and then old as what the gods made me, on the land where the gods put me." He glanced at me and then turned back to his people. "THAT'S ALL. You all kept bringing me complicated wild women, you wanted . . . ah, why would I of all people turn *terrorist*? Does that even make sense?!" He rubbed his sweaty face with his rough hand.

"Why don't you stop with the hysterics? Tell us what happened," a woman in the crowd shouted.

"Otherwise what?" DNA asked. "If I don't explain will my own *village* cast me out?"

"You are all over the clan networks," an old man said. "They will come for you, son."

"Only if someone here tells them I'm here, Chief Mohammed," DNA said. "I'm not a terrorist." He turned to his mother. "Mama, I'm not a terrorist. I only want peace." He turned to his brother. "Gololo, you're one of Nigeria's top investigative journalists and you're wrong."

As he told his people what happened, I pulled the sleeves of my shirt over my wrists and straightened my long dress to cover my metal feet. I adjusted the black veil I'd wrapped over my head and then I hoped for dear life that when their attention finally shifted to me, as it inevitably would, they wouldn't decide I was an abomination worse than a desert djinn and try to beat me to death as people had sought to do in the Abuja market.

I waited.

———

DNA was quite the storyteller, thankfully. They did not try to kill me.

All the time he spent alone with his steer in the desert, thinking and not using words, must have sharpened his usage of them when it was time to speak. He told of the incident in the farmer town. He pulled his people in. He enchanted them. He softened then opened their minds. By the time he finished weaving yesterday's violence into the tapestry, I'd relaxed. No one who'd truly listened could dispute that he'd been wronged.

That night he stayed with his brother and his brother's

wife. They had me stay with his mother. As I wondered and wondered what DNA was talking about with his journalist brother, his mother wondered about *me*.

"Don't worry dear, you can undress. It's just you and me."

I was holding up the long white sleeping garment she'd given me. I'd been shown to a tiny wash tent, where I bathed in privacy. No one saw my body. But now, she was looking at me, frowning.

"I'm really private," I said. "Can . . . can you maybe . . . ?"

She kissed her teeth and turned around, picking up her tablet. I removed my clothes and quickly slipped into the night dress.

"I'm an old woman," she said, her back still to me. "But I'm not blind. I've been in this world longer than you."

I pulled the nightgown to cover my legs as much as possible. My arms however were in full view. "I didn't want to scare you," I said.

She turned to face me, looked me up and down and said, "My son has returned without his cattle and with a woman who is not a woman."

"I'm a woman."

"*Can you lie with a man?*"

"Of course."

"Have you lain with my son?"

"I just met your son today. Hours ago."

"Yet he brings you to meet his family. You're special to him."

"It was just timing. Coincidence."

"No such thing as coincidence."

"Trust me. It's a coincidence."

"We used to think he was struck with sukugo, a wandering spell few ever recover from. My son has never brought a woman to the village. Never."

"These aren't normal times," I muttered.

"And what are you doing here? The way you speak this English tells me you're not from the north." Before I could answer, she held up a hand. "Forget it. You don't have to explain to me. Get some sleep, robot girl."

I smiled. I liked his mother. I lay on the mat and was asleep within seconds.

———

Someone was shaking me awake. I opened my eyes. It was still dark, but someone was holding a small dim light, a mobile phone. I gasped and tried to move away. *I'm dreaming.* Whoever was standing over me was wearing a veil, like the ones I liked to wear.

"Relax, eh!" she hissed.

"It's me," DNA said as I realized he was right beside whoever it was who looked like me. She held the light to her face. It was his sister Wuro.

"And me," she said. "But I'm going to pretend to be you."

"What?"

"AO, come. The Elders have to speak with us *now*. Get dressed. Then we have to *go*."

"Why?"

"We can't stay here."

"They're coming," his sister said.

"The other clans," DNA said. "Someone couldn't help himself. Herself. Themselves. Someone talked. Then the news probably travelled fast."

His brother rushed in carrying what looked like a large raffia basketball. He shoved it in DNA's hands. "Your two remaining cattle are at South End, waiting. They're coming from North End."

DNA and his brother paused, both their hands on the raffia ball thing.

"You really think it'll come to that?" Wuro asked, adjusting the veil on her head.

His brother nodded. And more unspoken words passed between them. DNA hugged the ball to his chest and turned to me. "Change of plans."

"I assumed," I said.

CHAPTER 9

Elders

The village's women had woven the entire structure from palm tree raffia. A building the size of a large living room that could easily and quickly be collapsed and folded and placed on the back of a camel when the time came to move on. Wherever they stopped, it was always placed in the center of the nomad village (which was about a quarter mile in diameter) and thus the hardest place for outsiders to get to if they ever found the village.

We met the Elders there. Inside it smelled strongly of oud and where it was warm outside, it was cool inside thanks to a solar air-conditioner sitting on the far end. It was well-lit because of the openings in a circle at the top that allowed sunlight to shine in as long as the sun was out and up. Inside, five Elders waited. Three were women, two men, all were quite tall and thin, and all were old. They wore traditional white nomadic robes. They motioned for us to sit down on the raffia floor. I was very conscious of them watching my legs and I quickly sat and covered them up with my long skirt.

"No time for introductions," one of the women said. She was clearly blind, her milky eyes unmoving. She had a motion sensor sitting on her shoulder like a green beetle. I could see two of the red dots it projected in front of her and to her right. "Dangote Nuhu Adamu," she said in a soft voice. "Are you telling the truth? You acted in self-defense?"

"I am and I did," he said.

"If you are lying, then you've pulled your family, your *village* into shame," she said. "Because we are going to defend you."

"I understand," he said. "I'm no terrorist. Almost all my cattle were brutally killed in that village. The people there were angry because of some other boys who had done terrible things. We're not all the same. Let's be honest, some herdsmen *have* become terrorists. All of us here can name relatives or men we know who left and . . . turned. The desert keeps creeping south, the storm keeps raging. Herdsmen give up their cattle and turn. But NOT ME. I am DNA. I only want a simple quiet life, and I love you all. I would *never* bring shame to you. Never."

"Who's this girl?" one of the male elders asked, pointing a gnarled finger at me. It was always men who asked this.

"I am called AO," I said. "I'm from—"

"What's your real name?" he asked.

I paused, narrowing my eyes at him. What did my "real" name matter? When my parents named me, they were naming the normal child they'd hoped I'd be despite what the doctors told them. "Anwuli Okwudili," I said.

"Eh, what does it matter?" DNA asked. "She says her name is AO, we should respect that."

"It all matters," the man snapped. "Look at this one's body. These Igbo people hold nothing sacred. They'll sell anything."

I got to my feet. "I didn't sell—"

"We have to go!" DNA said, also getting up. He picked up the raffia ball. "Look, Elders, AO and I survived terrible things less than forty-eight hours ago. Whatever you hear, know that we both just wanted to be allowed to *be*."

"Shut up and WAIT," the blind woman shouted. "Mahmoud, tell them!"

Possibly the youngest of the elders, Mahmoud was a tiny wrinkled man who held his gnarled walking stick on his lap as he spoke. "Where will you go now?" he asked.

"I don't know!" DNA said. "Away from here, before there's tribal madness!"

Mahmoud looked up at us for a long moment and then said, "Go and see Baba Sola, first."

At the mention of the name, all the elders started nodding vigorously and whispering, "Yes, go," "Fine idea," "He will know."

"You want us to go into the Red Eye?" DNA gasped. He looked at the raffia ball he carried.

"It will at least hide you," the blind woman said.

"We aren't trying to get rid of you," the man with the cane said. "We're *protecting* you."

"Your sister has already left the village," the blind woman said.

"Some are following, but not all," Mahmoud said, looking at his mobile phone.

"You should go," the blind woman said.

"And none of this is coincidence," one of the other elder women added, pointing an index finger in the air. "That one with her *wahala*, you with yours, and then meeting just after, during these times . . . yes, definitely go see Baba Sola!"

"OKAY," DNA said. "OKAY."

We started to leave, but I turned back. "There are some things that truly are just inevitable," I said.

"We understand that," one of the women said. "We all do, and that's why we live out here. We don't plant seeds for government money; we don't participate. But you have, my dear. *You* have. See your body? You may have had reason, but you are part of it, like it or not. Somehow he is, too, though he lived his life trying to stay out of it. We will pray for you both. But please, and we mean no insult by this, get out of our village."

I nodded and let DNA lead me to the opening of the portable village hall. He turned back one more time, "If none of you ever hear from me again, know that it is because you've sent me and this woman to a mad man."

"Sometimes madness is the best path!" Mahmoud called after us.

———

There were over 200 cattle outside the village, yet DNA was able to locate his two within minutes. It certainly helped when they rushed to us the moment he stood amongst the cattle and whistled. The two steer had small red bundles strapped to their backs.

"Oh thank you, mama," DNA said when he saw them. "Maybe we aren't about to die." He pushed the raffia ball between them.

"What?"

He turned to me and just grinned. " Let's go."

We left the village quickly, not daring to look back. My head throbbed intensely but not to the point where I needed to say anything. It faded the moment we were about a mile from the village, a similar distance to when it had begun as we arrived. Something about DNA's village triggered my headache. DNA stopped walking. The steer and I stopped, too. He looked back the way we came, slightly out of breath, and then at me.

"I hope your sister is okay," I said.

"My sister thrives on trouble." He laughed. "She's my sister." He shrugged. "She's not you."

I nodded, "That's a good thing." We both chuckled nervously.

"I think we're safe," he said.

"The clans don't have drones?"

"Oh they have drones, yes. But we can rest for a few minutes." He went to GPS and pulled a small square from one of the pack. He unfolded and unfolded it and shook it out. We sat down on it.

"Why is everything from your family red?"

"That's our color," he said. "People identify us by it. Other families have patterns, but my father, he just loves the color red."

"It makes me think of . . ."

"I know. Just look at the sky. It'll distract you."

I looked up. There were a few clouds, but more importantly, there was a slight haze of dust now. I shuddered at the thought of where that dust was blowing in from. *Jesus, are we that close to the Red Eye*, I wondered?

"We were lucky, but the fact that the clans didn't set up a perimeter of lookouts and even drones around the village tells me that they didn't really believe I was there," he said. "Which means we might still run into some of their scouts."

"Can your family update us on what happens?"

"No," he said. "The networks and groups are full of clan spies, people's accounts can be hacked. They'll be watching the accounts of all my relatives."

After a few minutes, I asked what had been nagging at me since we'd left, "Did they really believe you?"

"My sister, yeah. Maybe my mother," he said. "My brother? No. The Elders, mostly, yes. Everyone else? Definitely not. My reputation in the village, well, people think I'm strange, that I'm too much of a traditionalist. Like my embracing the solitary herdsman life was an excuse to get many young wives, avoid so-called real work . . . or be a terrorist. They've been waiting for something like this."

My shoulder flared hot with pain, and I stopped walking.

"What's wrong?"

"My arm. It hasn't been right since yesterday. Someone smashed at it with a brick."

"Can I see?" he asked.

I shook out my arm as I moved a step away from him. "It's fine," I said. "Nothing we can do about it out here, anyway." We looked at each other for a moment. "I'm just a really private person," I added.

"Hmmm, okay." He stepped back, raising both of his hands. "I understand."

I nodded, still rubbing my shoulder and bending and straightening my arm as much as I could. We continued on, and for several minutes he kept looking at me. He didn't think I noticed, but I did. An hour later, we reached a Noor. They looked nothing like how I'd imagined them. I thought they'd be like the windmills back home with the long sleek white base and the three-blade horizontal rotor. But Noors were monstrously huge, about the size and width of two football fields. Made of sand-colored most likely carbon-fiber plastic or glass fiber, these turbines were helical, and lay horizontally on the desert floor.

"They look sort of like strands of DNA," I said as we made a wide berth around it. DNA gave me a loathsome look, and I chuckled. He'd clearly heard this before. The wind had begun to howl around us and, surprisingly, it was only the wind that I heard, not the turbine. "They're so quiet," I said.

"What does it matter?" he asked. "The wind makes noise for everyone." He pointed to the northern end of the turbine. "You stand there, even a half mile in front of it, and the wind funneling through for energy will tear you apart because the helix accelerates it on its way out."

I squinted. The land in front of the turbine was flat and looked made of smooth stone.

"Do they all face the same direction?"

"The Noor south of the Red Eye, in this part of the desert, all face North South," DNA said. "That changes when you get farther in and when you travel east or west. They're drawing the wind from the storm and the storm moves in a circle, like a hurricane. *Ya'allah*, I hate imagining how much power Ultimate Corp harnesses from each and every Noor. They send all that energy wirelessly to wherever they want. And no one knows exactly where. Some place has lights because of these. There's a reason they are called "noor," which means "light" in Arabic."

"*Na wao*," I said. "Never knew that." But why not make some money off of a disaster? If they'd been the first to think up the idea, they deserved the wealth they made. But seeing a Noor up close like this, the enormity of the turbines, so many of them, all to profit from a disaster, how could that kind of thing be good? And how the hell had they built them? The helix structure didn't just harness the wind, it maximized the wind by containing it. The traditional designs might have been able to withstand the extreme winds of the Red Eye, but these helix designs were able to intensify the Red Eye's power and then harness it.

As the winds strengthened and the swirling dust increased, I moved closer to DNA. GPS and Carpe Diem instinctively trotted closer to us both. The sun was still out and relatively viewable, but it wouldn't be for long.

CHAPTER 10

A Failure

We'd passed two more of the monstrous Noors, both times while at a safe distance of a half-mile or so and never in their draft path. And even then, we could feel the strength of the accelerated winds blasting out their north-facing ends. And the sands were nearly unbearable, at least to me. GPS and Carpe Diem had their heads down but otherwise seemed okay, and DNA had wrapped his veil over his face but he didn't slow his gait. Until this moment.

"It's going to get very bad soon," he said, switching on his anti-aejej armband. Immediately, the sand that had been scraping at my clothes dropped and the four of us were in a tight bubble, protected from the sand. The barrier reached less than a foot above my head and inches from around us. If he'd waited this long to turn it on, its battery power must have been limited.

"Better?" he asked me with a smile.

"Much."

"You looked like you wanted to die," he said.

"Thought I was going to," I muttered.

We walked for another twenty minutes. Though the storm appeared to be close, for a long time, it seemed to stay in the same place as we walked toward it. It was *that* huge. The winds decreased here and he switched off his anti-aejej. While the storm lurked near yet far, we came across another menacing thing: The charred remains of an Ultimate Corp warehouse. Like the head of a great desert djinn, it loomed at the end of a parking lot whose asphalt was covered with a layer of shifting sands.

"Whenever I see this place, I think 'failure'," he said, patting Carpe Diem and GPS on their sides as he glared at the warehouse. "The biggest business out here is with the *small* people—nomads, people escaping, people hiding, the people of the desert have the biggest black market in the world. *Not* Ultimate Corp."

As we crossed the parking lot, I squinted at the warehouse. It looked like it had burned long ago, though I could have sworn I still smelled smoke. Minutes and about a half mile later, the winds grew strong and dusty. Somehow, the smoky smell of the burned warehouse withstood the winds for the moment.

"What happened there?" I asked. "Never heard of a warehouse in the north. And it's so close to the Red Eye." Across the empty parking lot, where a road ran into the distance, was a large sign with the Ultimate Corp logo, a stylized outstretched blue hand. Several chunks of the tiling had fallen off and shattered to pieces below.

"For a while, even Ultimate Corp tried to get in on business with people living in the Red Eye," DNA said. "They had these crazy delivery drones that could fly through the wind in the Red Eye. But they couldn't compete with the black market. Especially when thieves kept breaking into the warehouse and waylaying delivery drones, then reselling the stolen goods. Ultimate Corp tried to fight back; we call that day The Reckoning."

"Wait, was it that day when those desert black marketers ambushed those Ultimate Corp delivery drones?" I asked. "I saw coverage of that back home! It was the first time I ever saw

people of the desert who weren't, no offense, Fulani herdsmen
terrorists."

DNA looked deeply annoyed. "We aren't terrorists, it's
those stupid men who sold off or lost their steer. And no one
attacked those delivery drones. The Reckoning happened because Ultimate Corp tried to fight black marketers on their
own turf." He laughed. "So so stupid and arrogant. Afterwards,
all their employees fled and none came back."

"There was no Ultimate Corp warehouse on the news or
anywhere else."

"Of course not. How would it look to know that Ultimate
Corp was trying to do business with the 'wild people' living
in the Red Eye. But they were. Those drones that could move
through the wind, whipping sand and dust. They tried to use
those to attack desert people. That's when everything went to
shit."

"Interesting," I said, looking back at the warehouse. It must
have been a battlefield back then.

"We come from dust, to dust we all return, even failed Ultimate Corp projects."

We spread the red cloth right in the middle of the parking
lot, using stones we found littered around the place to hold it
down. And there we ate a heavy lunch from the food packed
for us. He used his small capture station to draw cool water; it
was small but still much bigger than the one I had. Mine certainly couldn't have drawn enough water in minutes to slake
ours *and* the steer's thirst. Even with the clouds in the sky, my
personal capture station was the size of a keychain and would
only have drawn a few cups of water. The steer drank noisily
from the bag; thankfully, I'd taken water into my cup first. I
shuddered when I saw him drink his water after the steer. Fried
chicken, goat cheese, dates, something he called latchiri, some

kind of vegetable soup he called takai haako—by the time we finished, both our bellies were comfortably full.

"It's not so comfortable to eat when in the storm," he said. "So fill up."

I nodded. "Even now, I feel like three percent of what I ate was sand."

He laughed. "Get used to that."

Sitting there was eerie. Since I'd left my car, this abandoned warehouse was the first thing I'd seen that was like home. And it had an apocalyptic feel. When we'd passed the front doors, which were brown from the flames' heat, I noticed that they swung a bit with the wind. I wondered what we would find inside if we went in there. Would there be charred remains of people who couldn't escape? Or just a bunch of burned lawn chairs, mobile phones, jars of honey, clothes, warehouse things.

Fifteen minutes after leaving the warehouse parking lot, he had to turn the anti-aejej back on. We were back in the high winds, the sky was dark with dust and the looming storm finally fell on us. It blocked out the sun. It locked in the heat. It made hearing difficult. What a feeling it was to be there. No car. No nearby shelter. Only the sky above. Somewhere. I wished I could have photographed myself in this moment, maybe the photo would capture my conflicting feelings of vastness, smallness, freedom, and doom. But I'd left my mobile phone behind, along with any connection I had to the connected world. I was here. Only in the moment.

When a gust of wind strong enough to pass through the anti-aejej's barrier made us stumble, we paused, meeting each other's eyes. He quickly turned to the raffia ball he'd stuffed between the bundles on GPS's back. He tapped on it and the raffia relaxed. The upper part of the ball collapsed revealing tightly packed items inside. He picked up and threw something white and small at me. I caught it and held it up. What slowly unfolded in my hand looked like a piece of clear gelatin. "It's a mask," he said. "Put it on now."

I unrolled it more and held it up. It looked like it would fit comfortably over my face, but it had no mesh where the eyes, nose and mouth would be. "How am I supposed to breathe with this on my face?"

"Just put it on," he said. He was holding up his own now. "I live out here. I know what I'm doing."

I watched him press it to his face and ears. Now they looked covered in a thick layer of oily gel. I pressed mine to my face as he pressed masks over the faces and ears of GPS and Carpe Diem. The moment it was on my face, I felt it go from cool to warm like my own skin. Like it was alive. I frowned, slowly letting myself breathe. There was no resistance at all. I could also hear just fine.

"Without these masks, you won't last long," he said, helping GPS step into some kind of protective bright yellow jumpsuit. "Your face, ears, and lungs are now protected from the dust."

When DNA was done, I looked at GPS and Carpe Diem and stifled a laugh. They looked as if they'd dunked their heads in buckets of water. And Carpe Diem, in particular, didn't seem to like the mask because her eyes were wide with shock. With the tight yellow jump suits, they both looked like aliens. "Steer suits aren't cheap," he said. "If I had all my cattle, we wouldn't be able to go. I've never gone into the Red Eye with my cattle." He frowned. "Until now." He reached for the off switch of the anti-aejej.

"Wait!" I shouted. "You're turning it *off*?"

"Of course! You think an anti-aejej will be able to hold back Red Eye winds?" He laughed loudly and shook his head.

"Oh, no no no. Maybe for a few minutes, but this small solar thing's battery can't withstand that kind of weight for long."

Fumbling with anxiety, I wrapped my veil more tightly around my head, thankfully my heavy long skirt and a layered top were otherwise good for the dust storm.

"If you can't quite see me, then stay close to the cows," he said. "GPS will let you hold on to his horn."

Just before he clicked off his anti-aejej, I looked ahead. I could see where it shifted from high winds to near madness. *My God, we are going to walk into that. On purpose,* I thought. Yet again, I marveled about how much my life had crumbled in a matter of forty-eight hours. What I saw up ahead reminded me of footage people on the Mars colonies were always posting on their social network accounts. The cloud of dust looming ahead of us was monstrous, spanning the entire horizon and lifting to block out the sun. In a few minutes, it would be like the night. "How the hell do people *live* in that?"

DNA laughed. "Some people like the dark."

My heart was pounding in my chest. "Really?" My voice shook. *Why did I come out here? There are better ways to die,* I thought. But I didn't really want to die any more. I had no foreseeable possible logical future, but I didn't want to die.

"Who is this Baba Sola?" I asked. "Why can't he come out of it and meet us here?"

DNA's laughter was beginning to unnerve me.

"You're just asking that *now*?"

"It's never too late," I said, irritably.

He turned off the anti-aejej. The force of the wind would have knocked me over if it weren't for my ground grasping autobionic feet. I grunted as my body flailed a bit, then I leaned forward, sand slapping at my clothes. The mask was incredible. I felt nothing on my face, though I knew sand was grating at it.

I could breathe perfectly. Not one grain of sand got in my mouth, and I could look around without sand getting in my eyes. It was almost like wearing a diving mask underwater, except the gel perfectly fit my face and made dwelling in the dust almost like a natural state. Still, the steer didn't seem to like this "natural state"; they moaned miserably and crowded closer to DNA.

My feet were made to adapt to any terrain from icy to uneven gravel, and I want to say I walked more easily than DNA did. I mean, he wore only a pair of thin flip flops. However, this was more his terrain, and his gait was as smooth and unhindered and probably just as painless as mine. Then the sharp rocks graduated to sand and we were trudging up the first dune when the sand storm swirled around us. And still we kept walking, slowly, beaten by the sand. When we reached the bottom of the dune, the steer refused to go any further, simply sitting down, all pressed together as they groaned with confusion.

"Come on," DNA shouted. "They'll stay here. We go a little further."

"Why?" I asked.

"Because he is always just beyond the worst of it," DNA said. "That's what they say."

"Who is this guy?"

He shouted something in Pulaar and trudged on, leaning into the sandy wind. I followed him. I'd come this far, I would keep going. Plus, though the wind and sand whipped the exposed parts of my body and collected in the folds of my clothes, my cybernetic parts moved me on as if it were a clear sunny day with no breeze. Yes, these parts of me loved the desert and dust. My human parts were what suffered.

At some point, I grabbed his hand and his responding grip

was strong. We moved into it. I don't know how long it lasted, but I was in the dark and in that darkness everything disappeared, except me and what I was left with. Those men had had it coming, but so had I. I'd always had it coming. In the dark this was all clear. I emerged from the warm protective darkness of my mother's womb poorly made. A mess. And then years later, fate had unmade me. How dare I embrace what I was and wasn't, and build my self? *Arm leg leg arm head, I am my own Allah*, I thought in the dark. Three years ago, I'd made this argument to my ex-best friend Dimmy who was Muslim and he had slapped me for blasphemy. I'd never talked about it with him after that day, after that moment. And the idea had grown stronger in me. But I had a lot of nerve. And now I was in the dark.

The madness stopped. It stopped so suddenly that I will never forget the sight of it. *Shhhhhhhhhhhh*. That was the sound of every grain of sand in a thirty-foot radius suddenly stopping its tumbling motion and dropping. Both DNA and I were showered with sand, our feet and legs buried nearly to our knees. DNA coughed and stepped out of the mound, letting go of my hand. I looked up, seeing the clear blue sky above, the dust storm whirling outside the radius. We were in the eye of a tornado in a hurricane, or maybe it was the radius of a powerful anti-aejej.

"Fuck!" I shouted, kicking my way out of the falling sand trying to bury me.

"Quiet," he hissed, despite the roaring of the wind around us. And somehow above it all, I heard him. I shook sand from my skirts and hair and was just beginning to feel like the worst was over when I looked up. I shuddered and grabbed his hand, pressing close to him. He was already also looking up, and he responded by pressing close to me, too. "I could have happily lived my whole life without seeing this," he said.

Together, we waited for gods knew what. I noticed first. The fact that the storm seemed to be opening, expanding, widening, without shrinking or slowing down. And there was something that looked like a tent yards away. But how was that possible. Though it was fairly calm, it was still windy. And inside, the tent seemed to have a glowing heart. A fire.

"There," I said, pointing. "You see it?"

After a moment, he said, "Let's wait a few minutes."

I pulled DNA with me. "Come on. That's why we came here and you know it."

Reluctantly, he yielded to my pulling. "I don't know anything anymore."

I felt a tingle in my left arm and I let go of DNA to rub it. It seemed every body part that I had chosen was achy and warm. My legs, my arm, my bowels, there was even an ache at the top of my head where the implants were. It didn't make sense. I was alive because of logical science. I'd only been able to support myself back in Abuja and Owerri as a mechanic because of logical science. Up to this point, everything, wild as it was, made sense because it was all really just logical science. But now here I was in the middle of a sand storm looking at a tent with a warm fire burning in its bowels. None of what was happening right now in this moment was logical or scientific.

"Come on," I said. "Let's go meet this wizard and see what he has to tell us."

CHAPTER 11

Baba Sola

When we reached the tent, DNA stopped so abruptly that I ran into his back. "What are you doing?" I snapped.

"Never met him," he said. "But I've heard . . . stories. You're a southerner. You don't know."

True. But I wanted to. If there had ever been a time in my life where I wanted to meet someone like this, it was now. "DNA, you should be dead."

His eyes widened at me; my words had slapped him.

"You were there the day before yesterday, with all your best herdsman friends. You were in range. They shot and . . ." I licked my lips and had to push myself to be blunt. I felt dizzy before the words even came out of my mouth. "They shot and h-h-hacked your people dead. Except *you*. They didn't even seem to *see* you. You said it yourself."

"I've heard this man moves backwards in time or something," DNA said.

"Then we don't have to worry that much about him, do we?"

"Also heard that he's a white man who lives outside of whiteness."

I laughed. "Impossible."

"I don't know why they'd send me here."

"Because you're wanted, and maybe he can help."

"They also say he's the worst kind of sorcerer," he whispered.

"Okay, I need to meet this guy," I said, smiling. I lifted the brown tent flap and bent forward to enter. The flap was heavy and stiff like a tarp and it made a dull crackling sound as I pushed it aside. The moment I was inside, two things hit me: Stark stillness and silence. As if the chaos outside didn't exist. As if we'd stepped into outer space. The quiet was so dense that I instinctively opened my jaw wide, trying to unpop my ears. No change. It smelled of a mixture of incense, smoke, and sweat and it was comfortably cool.

The interior of the tent looked vastly larger than its exterior, plenty of space to stand up straight and walk in before arriving at the large fire. It burned logs of wood stacked in a two-foot-high tower, and though it burned brightly, its flames didn't scorch or even blacken the cloth above. And then there were the walls of the tent, they shuddered from the wind outside, yet somehow made not a sound and none of the air current entered this strange space.

He sat across from the fire watching us. He wore heavy black robes that covered every part of his body except his face and feet. I frowned. His feet were too close to the fire. "Ah, finally grew some balls, I see," he said. He spoke English with an accent I could recognize. Maybe it was some form of American.

"I don't have balls," I said, before I could stop myself. I hated that phrase.

"Not you," he said. He pointed at DNA. "Him. I don't know what *you* have."

I narrowed my eyes at him. There are times to bite back and times to hold your tongue. He nodded, resting an elbow on his bent knee. He motioned toward us. "Okay, o," he said. "Good. Sit. Remove your masks. We will talk unhindered."

I took my gel mask off with a snap, and it immediately shrunk to a palm-sized blob. I touched my face; the skin was soft and damp. We sat across from him, the fire between us. He was indeed a white man, Caucasian. His nose long and narrow, his lips thin, pink and smirking, his smooth head bald, his eyes some color that was not brown, the fire made it hard to tell exactly what color. His pale yet slightly sun-touched skin made him seem to glow in his black robes.

He could have been sixty or three hundred years old. However, it wasn't his physical features that made me wonder if I should have left the tent flap shut. It was how close he sat to that fire. Even from where we sat, several feet back, it was hot. He was inches from it, his foot maybe two inches.

I could hear DNA whispering to himself beside me in Pulaar. Most likely praying. I chuckled to myself. There was no room or reason for prayer here. Whatever was going to happen to us now would happen, and probably with the permission of the gods.

"D-N-A the herdsman from nowhere," he said grandly, looking at him. "And A-O the auto mechanic from Abuja."

"You knew we were coming?" I asked.

He held up something that might have been a very ancient mobile phone. It was small and black, but thick. It looked like a piece of soap. He flipped it open, and its screen was barely a two inch square. "I get messages just like anyone else." He giggled as he flipped it shut with a loud *thock!* "They're coming for *both* of you, you know?" he said. He sat back, straightening his robes over his bent leg. He wiggled his toes with delight at the fire. He was a tall man, so his feet were large and spatulated. I noticed that they were dusty and his toenails were nicely manicured. So strange. "Ah, yes, I just figured I'd catch up with you two before the rest of Nigeria does."

"Catch up with us? *We* came to *you*," I said.

"AO," DNA hissed. "Don't . . ."

Baba Sola raised a hand. "Let her talk, let her talk, women need to talk. They are most useful when they talk. If we don't hear them, the universe suffers." He chuckled, and in that chuckle I knew, despite his words, he looked down his nose at women. He looked down his nose at everyone. "Yes, let this one talk. Yes, you found me. That's exactly how it went. And the world will find both of you. But not until I am done taking a look and marking this moment. Marking this *story.*" He raised a hand and suddenly there was a small cigarette in it. No not a cigarette, a joint. He leaned forward and touched it to the fire and then he took a deep pull. He slowly exhaled and the smell filled the tent.

I glanced at DNA and his face was pinched. He clearly wanted to complain and knew he should not. "Are you going to share that?" I asked. DNA stared at me and I shrugged at him. "Bad luck to break the cypher, or so my grandmother said."

"Your grandmother smoked this stuff?" DNA asked.

I rolled my eyes. Irrelevant things were even more irrelevant in a wizard's tent.

Baba Sola held it out, and I had to lean onto my knees to get it. I enjoyed marijuana once in a while, especially when I was in pain. And something told me that this was not the kind grown on corporate farms with corporate pesticides and corporate genetic modifications. This would be organic and very kind. DNA gave me a hard look as he watched me bring it to my lips. A joint from a sorcerer in a tent in the middle of a dust storm the day after I'd killed five men with my bare hands. I took a deep deep pull.

The smoke filled my lungs and within seconds, the world bloomed around me. Opulent, vibrant, and churning wilder than the winds outside. Yes, this was wizard's brew. I exhaled, and it was like I was exhaling the world, new and refreshed. It shifted and turned before me on its own axis. I frowned, unable to look away. I held the joint out to DNA and his frown deepened. "I am a Muslim," he said, disapprovingly.

"And you're a murderer in the tent of a wizard," I told him, my words leaving my lips with the smoke, smooth and cool like water.

"No," he simply said, and I shrugged. The world was breathing all around me. I inhaled and exhaled and it was like I was breathing with it.

"The world isn't all about you, AO," Baba Sola said.

"Yet the world's after me," I muttered. I took another puff and handed it back to Baba Sola.

Baba Sola paused, looking at DNA. "You sure?"

DNA shook his head.

"Ah-ah, he dey try, but what will be is what is, eventually," Baba Sola said, taking two more puffs before putting it out in the sand beside him. "Mister DNA, you've waited so long for a wife who adheres to tradition that you have surpassed the age when it is traditional to find a wife. You've fallen from the tradition you fight so hard to stay in."

The irony of his words was like someone lightly running a finger over my armpit; I couldn't hold back my laughter. I guffawed loudly and the sound of it made me guffaw even harder. DNA frowned at me. "You're high," he said.

"I am!" I shouted, pressing my hands to my mouth, giggles still escaping. *In a wizard's tent*, I thought and this nearly sent me to the moon with fresh laughter. I pinched my nose. Both Baba Sola and DNA watched me. For how long, I will never be able to tell you. But by the time Baba Sola spoke again, I had calmed down and was staring at the shuddering tent walls thinking they looked like the fists of people outside punching it. I wondered if those people outside would soon come in. And what they'd do to all of us.

"And you," Baba Sola said.

"Me?" I asked, looking at him. A white man in black robes who glowed like he had studied his craft with talent and skill for decades. I didn't believe in sorcerers, jujuwomen, witches and wizards until this moment. *I believe now*, I thought. *What will happen to me? To both of us? Maybe it's bigger than that.* I paused at this last thought, my eyebrows going up.

"Yes, you," Baba Sola said, his smile broadened as if he knew what had just cracked open in my mind.

"You fled into the desert and are now following a man. As is tradition."

Now it was DNA's turn to snicker. I wanted to slap him, but a part of me also wanted to snicker, too. The world was no longer the world.

"You're both here because this is a meeting," he said. "You've arrived at the same place from different places. I've been here before, I'll be here again. But neither of you will. What I can give you I've already given."

We both looked at each other, afraid to say what I was sure we were both thinking—that juju from this man would be real and true. The type our grandfathers referred to using one word, "abomination." Both of us leaned forward, listening.

"I had a friend who was a yam farmer in the east. *Ndi* Igbo," Baba Sola said.

I blinked at the phrase and just let it go. This white man in the desert was the real thing, nothing like those who'd come before wanting to colonize, appropriate, seize, and destroy. He was a white man who traveled and shared and learned and laughed and observed. Maybe he *did* live backwards. He probably knew a thousand languages. He probably spoke Igbo better than I could.

"He told me that long ago, two farmers went into the jungle hoping to escape the hard lives they were living on their farms. They met each other on the third day. It was as if the jungle was playing with them, leading them this way and that, deeper and deeper. It would show one a leopard, and he would flee. It would show the other a python, and he would flee even farther into the jungle. Neither was terrified enough to recapture his senses and return home to his good, not so bad life.

"Until that day when they met. By this time, they were each covered in red mud, because it had rained every day they'd been in the jungle. Their bellies were full of roots, wild yam leaves, and roasted bush meat they'd each found and consumed. Their eyes had adjusted to the darkness of living below the jungle's canopy.

"Now, when two farmers meet, normally, one will conquer the other. Farmers are territorial by nature. They cannot coexist on the same land. But this day, there was no fight to the death or battle of well-chosen words. The men could see with the clarity of the jungle and the purity of their purged minds. They hadn't heard the voices of their wives in days. And so they sat. They built a small fire. They talked of many things. These two men were never seen again after that night. Though some say, they both returned home to their wives and families and lived such rich lives that no one recognized them as the same men."

Baba Sola leaned back on his hands and crossed his feet at his ankles as he looked at us, clearly satisfied with himself.

"What's that story got to do with *us*," I asked. DNA nodded vigorously beside me, equally irritated.

"Your generation has lost the art of the proverb, the gift of wordplay, the science of fiction, the jujuism of the African," he said, picking up the joint he'd placed on the sand beside him. He brought out a match and flicked its tip aflame with his nail. He threw it in the fire, relit the joint from the fire and took a deep pull. He exhaled smoke, and I stifled the urge to cough. Despite the fact that we were in the middle of a whipping whirlwind, it smelled like we were suddenly in a tiny poorly ventilated room, and that room was filled with smoke; not marijuana smoke but the kind that rises from burning wood. Beside me, DNA started coughing. "Heh, amateur," Baba Sola said. "Can't even take the second-hand."

"I take what I want to take," DNA said, his cough subsiding.

Baba Sola laughed. "Only God knows everything in life," he said with a smirk, as if he didn't believe there was a God at all. "But I know plenty. Boy, give me your hand."

I realized DNA and I were still holding hands. All this time, we'd been holding hands. I hadn't even noticed it. Maybe it was the effects of the marijuana. Whenever I smoked it, time jumped in erratic unpredictable ways. One moment I was looking out the window, the next I was sitting on the couch with no recollection of the few seconds it took to turn, walk, and sit. I quickly let go of DNA's hand, for some reason embarrassed. DNA held my eyes for a moment and then turned to Baba Sola and leaned forward, his hand held out.

Baba Sola took another puff of his joint, held it between his lips and took DNA's hand as he gazed into DNA's eyes. "Some Yoruba like to put charms beneath the skin, but somehow I've always felt that was kind of primitive. It's like putting a computer chip under the skin instead of using nanotechnology to grow it right into the ribonucleic acid or just strong psychic energy from a travelling man like me." He leaned forward and roughly pulled DNA closer.

"What?" DNA asked, his voice shaky. I wouldn't have wanted to look into the sorcerer's eyes like that either.

"I don't think there's much I have to say to you. *But* I will say this: You're no king. You're no leader. You're just a herdsman. That's good. But you *listen. Listen.* And when they come," he leaned in. "Know. Your. Worth." With each of those last three words, he shook DNA as if he were trying to wake him up.

"What are you talking about," DNA whispered.

"You are not a herdsman, then?" Baba Sola said, letting go of his hand.

"I am, yes, but . . ."

"Then shut up," he said. He took another puff from his joint and, as he blew the smoke out, he added, "Just remember my words. I don't need your response to them." Baba Sola raised his chin, his attention on me now. His eyes were blue. A cold, frozen, blue, like those of a mysterious cat. He took another pull at his joint and held it.

With each and every word he spoke, came a puff of the heady smoke. It was as if he were speaking a spell. "You, my dear, you've been fucked with enough. Time for you to see beyond yourself and fuck the world. Make it see a new day." He sat back and dismissively waved a pale hand at us. "I'm blessed to have witnessed the both of you in person, but it's time for you to be on your way. They're coming."

"Who?" DNA asked.

"Everybody," he said. He was fading and the fire was fading and soon the tent began to fade, too. We both jumped up.

"Hey!" I shouted at the disappearing Baba Sola. "What do we do now?"

He laughed. "Not my story to tell." He was gone.

And we were outside.

"Quick! Put your mask on!" DNA said. I was still carrying mine in my left hand, and quickly I pressed the gel to my face and ears. When I looked up, I saw the eeriest thing. The sun saw me and decided to hide, even as the dust covered it up. The sun *moved*. Swiftly. And then it was hidden behind the dwindling edge of the swirling storm. And it took the light before the dust could roll and swirl in. The light faded as Baba Sola had faded, quickly, suddenly, for no reason.

I grabbed DNA's hand as both sand and storm fell back on us.

"Your steer?" I shouted over the noise of the storm.

He looked around, shielding his eyes with his other hand. "GPS," he called. "Carpe Diem, to me!" I wanted to hold up my left hand and shine the small light in my fingernail around us because it was so dark, but instinct told me to wait and keep holding on to DNA.

"Urooooo!" The sound came from right behind me and I jumped, whirling around. I felt the cow push past me to nuzzle against DNA's arm. And GPS stood right behind her. I could see this because it suddenly wasn't so dark anymore. A piercing floodlight cut right through the dust. The drone shining the light blasted through the dust so strongly that it created a momentary funnel that reached the clear star-filled sky. *It's nighttime?* I franticly wondered. How long had we been in that sand storm with the sorcerer? Maybe it was the marijuana and its time jumps.

The dust and wind swooped back in and closed the opening to the sky and I held on to DNA and one of GPS's horns for dear life. The powerful lights from the drones flooded all around us, helicopters zipping just above us like alien ships. But somehow, they didn't *see* us. Was it some of Baba Sola's lingering juju? DNA's weird ability to be unseen as he had been in that town? A loophole in my country's elaborate surveillance system? Maybe they didn't see us for all these reasons. Technology always fails eventually, and juju is made to succeed.

We snuck right past an entire line of soldiers—a herdsman wanted for murder, a woman mechanic wanted for murder, and two steer who'd survived attempted murder. The soldiers had somehow surrounded us, yet been unable to find us. To speak might have changed this, so when GPS blundered to the right and then forward, as if he knew where to go, we did, too. The sandy wind bit at and buffeted us about and for several minutes, it felt like being lost in a furious stinging sea. The wind was behind us, then in front of us, then beside us, but mostly beside us. I could feel it trying to tear at my clothes, grating at my flesh, pushing for my organs, trying to take my breath away, threatening to whisk me away. We moved slowly but steadily, shoulders hunched, heads down.

The veil of the Red Eye began to lift, and now it was mainly just wind we were contending with. "GPS really knew where he was going," I shouted over the wind, finally feeling able to let go of both him and GPS's horn.

"It's not my first time trusting him," he said. "Now you understand how he got his name. If you let him lead the way, he'll always lead you out of the Red Eye. He hates it."

"Handy and good friend to have," I said, patting the animal on his side.

"Yes," DNA said.

We emerged into a field of dried grass, near the warehouse. We'd made it through the fields and were just about to cross the remaining hard pan to the parking lot when we heard it behind us. A loud roaring. My heart sank. We didn't stop or look back until we were running across the parking lot, right into the glass doors of the abandoned warehouse we'd passed earlier.

"*This* is why we stay away," I heard DNA say as I put a hand to the dirty glass door. It opened smoothly, almost as if the hinges were oiled or removed. Why would they leave a warehouse door unlocked, even if there was nothing inside? And though the sun had set long ago, the door was warm to the touch. The noise continued behind us and finally, I looked back. What I saw made me want to abandon all hope.

Soldiers were setting the field of grass we'd just run through on fire. It didn't take much and the wind provided even more fuel. There were about ten drones flying over it and spraying flames on the grass like water, aiming their fiery spray from south to north to avoid setting themselves aflame. What they spewed was thick, nearly solid flame that looked and heavily fell like lava.

"Why are they doing that?" I shouted.

Within minutes, desert grassland that had been untouched and unbothered for probably years, looked like a war zone. DNA was muttering in Pulaar again. I shook my head, trying to clear it. I was still high from Baba Sola's wizard marijuana and the field looked as if it were blooming and swirling, not being razed by swirling biting fires. The propellers from the many drones which, clearly, were fireproof, created miniature whirlwinds in the flames.

Then I noticed them. "DNA! Look! Look at them."

They came running about the edges of the flames, unbothered by the heat. Some even ran into and out of the fire. The soldiers were automated. Upon closer inspection, I could see that they didn't move like human beings at all. Their motions were fluid, perfect and measured to cover distance using the least amount of energy and time. They would soon find we were not there. Then they'd come here.

DNA flung the door open and it fell off the hinges, clattering to the ground. An old charred smell wafted out, but the terrified steer trotted right in, shoving past both of us through the double doors. DNA and I paused for a moment, looking at the flames and smoke rising in the fields. The fire's blazing light reached far enough to light the beginning of the Red Eye's churning winds of dust, some of the flames actually whipping into fiery whirlwinds.

"My family has never been a part of this," DNA said. "We stay out of the way of this kind of 'civilization.' Look at them coming here and just *doing* this. Burning everything. For what? You? Me? Who are we?"

I was barely listening. Whirls of flame, automated soldiers, drones, all the way out here. Since when could drones vomit flames? My God, I was in trouble. It felt ominous turning our backs on fields of fire to enter a burned out building.

CHAPTER 12

Charred Space

I will tell you about Ultimate Corp warehouses or you'll never understand the absurdity of the one we were in. First of all, no one knows where Ultimate Corp is actually based. Tracking its activities is tricky. It's like the software I use to scramble my location; you'll be misled all over the world. But you will rarely be led to Nigeria, itself, and *that's* where Ultimate Corp does much of its business.

Nigeria has its problems, but it is a wealthy country and so much of its people's truest wealth remains untapped because the rest of the world sees the entire continent as "war-torn," "diseased," and "poor." I'd never seen the inside of an Ultimate Corp warehouse, but they were all over southern and central Nigeria. To go on one of these warehouse tours was to come out with some serious complimentary swag. There were big lotteries for tours, and whole families celebrated when people won.

Also, when people on tours posted footage of what they saw, Ultimate Corp, with over a billion followers (even *I* followed Ultimate Corp), always amplified these posts. To go on a warehouse tour meant instant followers and appearances on blogs and in publicity stories. If you'd always wondered what it felt like to be instantly famous, get a tour of an Ultimate Corps warehouse.

From what I'd heard, it was truly worth it. Rows and rows and rows of thirty-foot high aisles, fully stocked with various goods from foodstuffs to electronics to cosmetics to everything a human being needed. Delivery drones were always local and these warehouses made it so that they never had to travel far to pick up items and deliver them. Thus, inside was like . . . well, a hive of drones.

Ultimate Corp warehouse roofs had launch and landing pads, and their advertisements boasted that these roofs, the sides of the buildings, and the land owned by Ultimate Corp were all green, covered with the super grass known as periwinkle ("peri," for short). Peri was sturdy, so drones taking off, landing, and driving on it didn't harm it at all. Its flowers were a soft periwinkle color, and its tiny leaves were light green and grew in an elegant fractal shape, so the plant itself was beautiful. It grew easily in even the worst soil, faster than any weed, and required little to no water, yet it held water like a succulent. And eating a cup of boiled, fried, or roasted periwinkle was more nutritious than a daily vitamin. It was so delicious and cheap, it replaced rice the moment Nigerians tasted it. Ultimate Corp had cultivated its own strain of periwinkle, harvested and distributed all over West Africa by the corporation and taxed by the government.

Everyone benefited, Ultimate Corp social networking influencers and spokespeople boasted. The corporation's slogan in Nigeria was even, "Family first." Ultimate Corp warehouses were known for giving out "excess" bags of periwinkle flour to those who came to the warehouse entrances at 5 PM and agreed to post a photo of themselves holding and smiling at their bag of "free" flour.

Few in the south spoke ill of Ultimate Corp. I never really knew how to feel about it. I bought most of the car parts for the shop from there; it was just the easiest and cheapest place to find what I needed. But it permeated every aspect of where I lived, and I'd never liked that part of it. Ads were everywhere, most roads and massive swaths of land were owned by the corporation, a lot of the smartest university students had their tuition paid by them and Ultimate Corp products even showed up in the local markets often cheaper than what locals could sell. I was torn, though I knew Ultimate Corp was a problem. In the end, I just focused on myself and how it affected my own life and in that way, I guess, I was able to live with Ultimate Corp's pervasiveness.

It was a helpful cog in a thriving Nigerian country, even with the disaster in the north. Nevertheless, I'd never heard *anyone* mention this or *any* warehouse in the north. And battle between the local Black Market and Ultimate Corp, "The Reckoning" as DNA had called it, had clearly been covered up in the news. No, not just covered up, erased. I'd never heard a thing about it and I was pretty attuned to national news. Nevertheless, a humongous charred edifice in the desert can only be erased by the desert, and the desert takes its time.

Inside, I held up my left hand's light to see ahead and the darkness seemed to swallow it. DNA used his phone to light the area around our feet, and we saw that soot already caked his sandals and my metal feet. GPS sneezed several times, and Carpe Diem kept snuffing as if she couldn't stand the smell. Walking inside the burned warehouse was to enter a huge black cave that could crumble in on itself at any moment. Every step we took was a crumbly grainy sooty risk. And the smell, my God.

"Maybe hiding in here isn't such a good idea," I said, coughing into my arm. "This whole building is probably carcinogenic. How's it still standing?"

"Sheer will," DNA muttered.

The place might as well have still been on fire, the smoky

smell was so concentrated. And it was cool in here, giving it an even greater feeling of entering the bowels of something dead. Above, there were holes in the vast stainless steel sheeted ceiling, blackened by soot, as if something had tried to cut its way in.

"Being in here is better than being out there, where all they have to do is burn us down," he said. "This place is already burned."

"They can more than burn us. Plus, they'll know we're in here."

He nodded.

"We're caught," I said.

"Hmm," he said, as we kept walking. He looked up at the aisles which were so burned you couldn't tell what had been stacked on them. "We should try and get some rest while we can," DNA said after a few moments. We were only nearing the middle of the place; that's how enormous it was. The sound of the fire blazing outside was loud enough to hear through the walls, but it sounded distant. There was no sound of anyone or thing trying to enter or land on top of the building, at least not that we heard. I was tired and Baba Sola's marijuana had left me ravenous, so I had no aversion to some rest. Plus, it was only a matter of time, so best to get our energy up.

"I'm going to chance something," he said. He brought out the anti-aejej. "There's a way we can get some true rest. But there's a price to pay."

"What is it?" I asked, going to Carpe Diem, who'd already sat down and gone to sleep right there beside one of the aisles. GPS was sitting, too, but he looked ready to jump up and flee at the slightest command.

"My anti-aejej has surveillance capabilities. It can detect movement and an electronic or digital signal for a mile radius.

So that would include the roof, but leaving it on, even for a few hours, will deplete the battery."

"Meaning, if we have to go into the Red Eye again, all we'll have are our masks?"

"The anti-aejej will have some energy, but yes, not much."

"It doesn't use solar to recharge?"

"How much sun is around here?" he snapped.

I frowned, pinching my chin. "What about wind? Can it recharge using that?"

He kissed his teeth, more deeply irritated. "Do I look like I can afford that kind of anti-aejej?"

We stared into each other's eyes, and I looked away when I felt the tears come and my heart begin to race. I looked at my hands and made two fists. My left shoulder wouldn't allow me to raise my left arm all the way, but I could still make two fists. "Sorry. So . . ." I cleared my throat and shut my eyes. "Well, we probably won't make it past them to the Red Eye anyway, so . . ." I sighed.

DNA switched on the anti-aejej's surveillance app. As we'd both suspected, nothing was trying to get in, hover above or dig beneath the burned warehouse. I wondered if they'd even left the fields of grass to keep burning. We settled in for some rest.

I was sad, scared, tired, and more than a bit angry. Everything smelled like smoke from both inside the building and outside in the fields. The winds made the place creak with every gust. Yet and still, I ate well. It had felt like only a few minutes, but according to DNA's anti-aejej and mobile phone, Baba Sola had kept us for nearly a day in his tent. How quickly they'd have found and disposed of both DNA and me if it weren't for his shenanigans. That said, a blend of the marijuana and not eating for so long made the day and half old leftovers the tastiest things on earth. The dates had started to dry, but they were sweet and wonderfully chewy. The fried chicken had grains of sand on it and had lost its crispness, but it just seemed like the perfect food for the moment. The water was warm, but so nourishing I'd had to sneak off twice to relieve myself.

After we ate, DNA retreated some feet away, spread another blanket, removed his shirt and lay down. I sat where we'd eaten and once I was sure he was asleep, I took off my skirt. Freeing my legs felt great. Wearing only my panties and top, I wrapped my skirt over my shoulders. I stared at the black wall, nothing in particular going through my mind for once. It was nice. As I stared, the blackness of the charred ceiling seemed to blend with the darkness of the space. Both of the steer were fast asleep, and I knew I should have been sleeping, too. But it was so cold in this dead place and the wizard's weed was still in my system, making everything too clear.

My chest tightened as I thought of my father. Sitting on the porch drinking his beer and reading headlines on his phone. Wondering about me. My mother sitting with her cat on her lap, a cat that looked more like a lion cub than a house cat, a cat who would only sit on *her* lap. Staring into space while she wondered about me. And my brother would be playing his talking drum, maybe hoping I'd hear them. I sniffled, longing for home in Lagos for the first time since I'd gone wild. It was like a burning stone deep in my gut, a pain I couldn't reach. I sighed loudly, imagining that I exhaled smoke, despite my skin feeling so cold. I looked over at DNA.

They were coming for us, so I went to him. He'd never have come to me. He'd curled himself tightly on the blanket he'd pulled from his bundle and pressed himself to the black wall. Not to enjoy its coolness but to get away from me. From everything. I'd breached one strange border the day before yesterday when I killed those men who'd tried to kill me, breaching another was not hard.

I touched his bare shoulder with my fingers. He didn't flinch away. I moved closer. He gathered me in his arms and pulled the blanket over us both. I let him touch those parts of me that were still soft, still flesh, still human and I sighed, smiling.

"I can see why you bother those men," he whispered, running a hand over my torso, again.

I frowned, pulling away. He pulled me back to him. I could have pinned him to the floor with one hand. I didn't.

"You're a woman despite so much of you being machine," he said. "I'm not a fool; I know you're very strong." He paused, his hand working its way down my belly. He brought his other hand forward, grasped the metal of my left thigh. He spread my legs. "I'm just not afraid of it."

I stared at him, surprised by his words. For the first time in my numerous dealings with men, I let a man take me without me saying a word.

━━━━━━

The anti-aejej's surveillance didn't ping. It detected nothing. I heard nothing. DNA heard nothing. GPS and Carpe Diem heard nothing. We were all asleep. But in my sleep, I had a feeling. That's what woke me up. I had a feeling. I'd been dreaming about my brother. He was sitting in a courtyard by the sea. Maybe it was New Calabar, maybe Lagos, maybe Accra, maybe Durban, maybe Dakar. What I knew was that it felt familiar, though I couldn't tell just how familiar. The sun was shining, and my brother was standing on the concrete of a courtyard at the edge of the ocean. He was wearing a white shirt, and he was sweating through it. His white pants were spotless. And he was playing his talking drums, his eyes closed, aware of nothing else. I was watching him.

Then I awoke to the talking drum of my headache. The moment I came to wakefulness, the headache stopped. I sat up. I had a feeling. I looked at DNA beside me, fast asleep. Exhausted. Carpe Diem and GPS were both still asleep, too. I looked up at the ceiling. I gasped. Sunlight was shining through the tears in the steel. We'd slept right through the night. Not three hours, at least six! The drums in my head started again.

I rubbed my temples and then quietly got up and dressed. I barely made a sound as I walked away from the three of them, past the burned aisles, down the charred entryway. To the front door.

CHAPTER 13

Here I Am

. . . And so here I was, leaving the warehouse. This wasn't the plan. We had no plan. My left shoulder ached a little as I slowly bent down and grasped a handful of sand with my right hand. I felt the grains rub against the metal of my cybernetic fingers, I could hear the grinding. I sifted the sand from my hand, letting it pour on my exposed cybernetic arm, grains entering the joints, wristlets, touching wire and circuit. The discomfort faded and I sighed, looking up. "Fucking Ultimate Corp," I whispered to myself, pressing fingers to my temple, trying to quiet the drums that would not be silenced.

Above, the sun spread across the sky like a jellyfish, brighter and more alive than it had ever been. And drones danced around its sunbeam tentacles like insects. About fifty of them, a swarm of mechanical giant bees. Their powerful propellers whirred and whipped, blending the air. Gathering all this hardware was probably why they took so many hours to come for us. How many parts of the world were now watching? Waiting to "accidently" see a slaughter, devising ways to monetize the moment as word spread and eyes signed on to watch. I wondered if our stories had been combined yet, "In two minutes, witness the reckoning of the murderess and the terrorist," "This Is What Too Much Technology Will Do," "Herdsman Terrorist Trapped in Old Building With Robot Lover," "Africans Gone Wild!"

We would be like the American football player who fled police in the white car that my grandfather was always laughing about. Or the Saudi president who was eventually captured in a hole in the ground. What happened to DNA and I would give people something to talk about, cheer on, rant about, hate-watch. Our plight would be distraction and opiate. The global public would hungrily gather and tune in to a public execution.

There was an army before me and I laughed to myself; were these government or were they private soldiers working for Ultimate Corp? Who knew anymore. From where they stood, on the farthest side of the parking lot, I could see that they were all humanoid drones. Whoever was behind this didn't want to risk any casualties beside me. They were all a dull gray with round heads and white swift moving feet. Their metal bodies were coated with something that made them shine and sparkle in the desert sun. All the better for visual effect. Only two miles or so north loomed the dusty beginning of the Red Eye. The air was dry, clear, and hot, like a machine nearby was working at maximum power. I took several steps away from the warehouse, onto the street.

"Here I am," I said, spreading my arms wide. "Come and get me!"

Several of them heard or saw me. A soldier held up a white hand and pointed my way. Theatrics for those watching. What did robots need to visually signal each other for? They merely needed to ping each other, if even that. The others started slowly trudging forward. There was a loud beep from above and all the drones started gathering closer together.

"What the heck are you doing?"

I whirled around to see DNA pushing open the glass door. Behind him crowded GPS and Carpe Diem.

"Go back inside," I snapped. "They don't have to get *both* of us!"

Instead, he stepped up and stood beside me. GPS and Carpe Diem trotted out and GPS immediately found some dry weeds growing through a crack in the doorway and started gnawing at them. The drones hovered low before us. I couldn't tell what kind of weapons they carried—guns, Tasers, tear gas, bombs. All I knew was that they had eyes and most likely all of Nigeria was watching, Nigeria and beyond. The soldiers were almost here.

"What do you want to do?" DNA asked.

I paused. The soldiers were halfway across the parking lot. The drones had stopped thirty feet above. "Nothing," I said. I was frowning to keep the tears out of my eyes. They would kill us. Were my parents and my brother watching? My few friends in Abuja? My stupid ex? Maybe not. Probably, though. I glared at the drones. Glared hard, imagining they could feel my rage. They had no right. NO RIGHT. I glared at the approaching soldiers. They were two thirds across the parking lot. The three in front of us had raised their left arms and pointed them in our direction. They had no faces, their heads white spheres.

"Anwuli Obioma Okwudili and Dangote Nuhu Adamu, you are both under arrest for murder."

Thoom. The surge of pain in my head was so horrible that I could have sworn I *heard* the headache. I knocked on my forehead with my knuckles. "Ugh, my God," I muttered.

"You still want to do nothing?" DNA asked.

One of the steer mooed.

"If you run," one of the soldiers said, "you will be shot. Please do not . . ."

I wasn't listening any more. I was looking. Not with my eyes. The pain in my head made me stop, listen and *look*. As I did this, I felt something larger than ever rupture in my head. Then a wet warmth with the pain like before. I stumbled forward. DNA was yelling something. I looked up at the approaching soldiers. One of the steer mooed again loudly behind us. But it was all like it was happening from a distance and I had my back to it.

The drones descended. The soldiers were feet away.

I looked at one of the soldier's sphere heads, the one closest to me. There was a camera eye behind it.

I went *in*.

I was walking down a slope so steep I couldn't help but run. I was falling. Tumbling. Into blackness like the vortex of a black hole. Echoes of my own voice, my shouts, my intakes of breaths. Reverberating as I fell down down, in in.

I came to a stop so abruptly that it took my breath away. When I looked up, thousands of red eyes were staring at me, clustered together like the seeds of a pomegranate. The rest I cannot describe except for the fact that I could *do* it. I heard Baba Sola in my head and he was laughing. *No one would give you the ability if you weren't expected to use* it, he said.

So I *did*. I used it.

I glanced at DNA who was looking at me with the saddest look I'd ever seen. The look of "It's been nice knowing you" and "This is going to hurt." The soldiers were yards away. The drones hovered feet in front and above us.

"This is your final warning," one of the soldiers said. The voice was automated. My government (or more likely Ultimate Corp) couldn't even give us the respect of a real human's voice before executing us.

"Stand down," I said. "All of you." I didn't shout, but I spoke loud and clear. Not for *them* (for *they* could hear me in my mind), for everyone else, those human beings watching and broadcasting. I was looking at all the red eyes and they were looking at me. It was as if I'd typed my words and then hit enter. Final. Clear. A command.

There was no moment of pause or processing. It was instant. The soldiers brought down their weapons. The drones retreated. I could literally *hear* human gasps of shock from somewhere; someone was shouting "What the fuck! How'd she do that? Na witchcraft now?!"

DNA was staring at me. His mouth agape.

"Everyone," I said. "You're watching? Good. Watch me do this." I grinned, looking into the eye of the drone before me. "Move away," I said to them. It was easier now. All those eyes. I laughed. We were getting out of here. Oh yes we were. And even better than that, we were going to make a hell of an escape because the government (yes, it was the Nigerian government) had been too afraid, lazy, underestimating, reliant on technology to send actual human soldiers.

"DNA, get ready," I said, turning to him. "Put the masks on GPS and Carpe Diem. And put yours on, too."

"What'd you do?" he asked, bringing the masks out. He looked stunned. How was I going to explain it all? The certain rupture and bleeding in my brain, the connection. Those headaches, had this been coming? How could I explain that I saw a whole universe that humans didn't even know they'd created? And that I was now connected to and could *control* it? Beyond the parking lot, I could see a wake of dust rising as the covered Jeep sped to us. It was one of the several that had brought the automated soldiers.

"My headache's gone," I said to DNA, grinning and snapping the mask on my face and ears.

The soldiers moved and made room for the covered truck to drive right up to us. It drove in a semi-circle and came around, its rear to us. The back doors opened and a ramp slowly lowered. We pushed GPS and Carpe Diem in, then hopped in the front, and it drove us right past all the standing soldiers and hovering drones. I poked my head out the window and called one of the drones to us. I could see through its camera as it flew above us. I laughed and sat down.

"What is going on?" DNA asked, the cockeyed grin still on his face. His left cheek was twitching. He leaned to the side and looked out the window behind us as the truck slowed. We were almost out of the parking lot, all the robot soldiers and drones behind us. Then *PAFF*, the white head of one of the soldiers blew off. Then another, and another. Then the drones fell one by one.

I was doing this. Overheating circuits, melting processors just by giving commands. The soldiers didn't fall, they simply sat down and did not move again. I stopped the truck and got out to watch. And to keep causing it. It was easy. But I still had to concentrate. DNA got out on the other side.

An audience was lost with each drone that fell. "Yes," I said, laughing. "Good bye." Another fell. "You are not entitled to watch." Another fell. "This is a show you will miss." Another fell. I laughed. The soldiers were sitting down and the world-wide public was being denied its bloody voyeuristic feast. And I was still standing. With places to go.

———

The drive across the burned field was smooth enough from last night's broiling and it would only be minutes before we arrived at the initial dust of the Red Eye. Already the Jeep was getting buffeted around by the wind.

"How'd you do that?" DNA asked yet again. I'd closed the

windows and despite the winds outside, it was strikingly quiet
in the truck. It reminded me of Baba Sola's tent.

"I . . ."

"Have you been able to do that all this time?"

"Of course not," I said. "I . . ."

"Was it Baba Sola?" he asked. "It was juju, wasn't it? Maybe
it was that weed you smoked or . . ."

I laughed. "You *really* have issues with cannabis, don't you?
It's just a *plant.*"

"You were controlling drones and robots with your mind,"
he said. He frowned at me. "Are you some kind of government
experiment? Like in the movies?"

"Shut up, DNA," I snapped. "I told you how I came to be
what I am. It was *my* choice. I have these headaches. Remember, I told you about those?"

"I do."

"I felt something in my head. I felt it . . ." I shuddered. "Tear
open. Right after the first man slapped me back in the market.
I could feel it. Then it tore more back there at the charred warehouse, and I could see something that I could *do.* Then I just
could do this." *And maybe getting slapped that hard broke something,* I thought. *And sometimes when something breaks, things
come out of the cracks.* I shuddered and I looked ahead. Here we
were again, the enormous wall of dust, dirt, and sand was rolling toward us like the end of our lives. I shuddered, again. "I
think. . ." I frowned, feeling dizzy for a moment.

"What?" he said, staring ahead. "What do you think?"

"It's so scary," I said, tears wetting my eyes.

"I know. No one ever gets used to the sight of it." He took
my hand. I squeezed it and sobbed, looking at the Red Eye.
"Don't look at it. This'll be better than going in with just an
anti-aejej. This truck should be made to withstand the wind,

it's probably weighted. It would be stupid to bring it out here if it can't take it. What did you think? Tell me about that."

And as I spoke, the great storm blocked out the sunlight we had left. I spoke fast because it felt like I only had seconds. "I think it started when that man hit me in the market. That's when I first glimpsed the *eyes*."

"Eyes?"

The truck was rocking now, but the winds didn't blow it away. We were still driving forward. It *was* made to endure the Red Eye. I hoped it was *well* made. The headlights switched to floodlight mode. They were solid beams of light in the dark chaos. In the back, Carpe Diem and GPS moaned softly, but they seemed okay. The truck remained relatively dust-tight. We wouldn't need to use the anti-aejej. I tapped the dashboard, which was all touch screen. I ran my hand over it and was able to do what I needed to do. "So easy," I whispered.

"You can keep controlling the truck?"

I nodded. "I just shut off the tracking that would tell them where we are." I touched the screen again and worked my hand in a circle. The satellite GPS was useless, but I still had one other tool. Up came a rudimentary thermal and motion scan of the area. The Red Eye's air currents showed as blue constantly moving lines. For miles around us was nothing that produced heat. Literally nothing. The land was windswept cracked earth.

"There," DNA said, pointing at the bottom of the dashboard.

"What is *that*?" I asked. The red shape was pretty big, miles long and wide and it was laid out in the strangest shape. "It almost looks like an infinity symbol."

"Not infinity," he whispered. "I know what that is." He grinned. "It has to be!" He looked at me. "If that's what I think it is, a lot of people actually *do* think that place is infinity, that it's everything. I think that's the Hour Glass! The anti-aejej protecting it must give off heat, that's why we see the shape so clearly."

"Wait, what? There's an anti-aejej that *huge*?! What for? Why's it in the middle of one of the planet's greatest disaster areas?"

"It's the biggest anti-aejej in the world and its *wind* powered," he said, almost proudly. "Ultimate Corp isn't the only one who knows how to harness the Red Eye's wind."

I squinted at the screen, noting just how big it *was*. Miles wide and two miles long. "There's no other way an anti-aejej could be that huge and maintain power. Has to be wind power here, yeah. But why?"

"The Hour Glass is the greatest city of Non-Issues the world has ever seen," DNA said. "It is legend. It's where people go to be found, to disappear, or to just be. There's law and order but there is no Ultimate Corp or Nigerian government."

"You sound like you really want to see this place," I said. "Why haven't you gone?"

"Look around," he said. "You think I'd travel into this on purpose?"

"Good point."

I sat back on the chair and just shook my head. I had never in a million years heard of such a place. "This is too much."

"Oh *now* you say that?" he laughed. "I was thinking the same thing a few minutes ago when you were using your *mind* to stop government weapons from executing us."

I sighed and closed my eyes. But when I did this, I saw a billion eyes looking back. I opened my eyes. *How the hell am I ever going to sleep*, I wondered.

"The Hour Glass isn't just *named* for its shape," he continued.

"It's also protected by a strong digital net that scrambles any sense of its location every hour on the hour."

"So it'll disappear from the GPS in an hour?"

"Maybe less," he said. "I don't know what time it is right now, but it's always at 1:11 in the Hour Glass, and then the count starts again ."

"So their time is always between 12:11 and 1:11?"

"Correct," he said. "But I don't even know why it's showing up on this GPS."

"Might be me," I said. "I was searching for any place in the storm we could run to."

He nodded. "I think we should try and make it there. It's six miles away."

I checked the time. It said 3:23 pm. So that gave us 48 minutes before the next wipe and it disappeared from the GPS.

"If this truck can follow the GPS, we can make it," he said.

"Okay," I said.

The front seats of the truck were made for humans, so they were at least cushioned. I made sure the truck didn't drive over twenty miles per hour, to stay on the safe side and give us a chance to rest for about a half hour. DNA napped, but I was afraid to even close my eyes. *What am I now?* I kept wondering. I could connect to all things online by wifi without an electronic mediator. *Was* I an experiment? To follow that theory meant going to some ideas I didn't want to approach. *Maybe I'm an accident.* I thought. *Or a glitch or a mutation.* Whatever I was, the whole world knew it now. No, I couldn't sleep a wink.

CHAPTER 14

Do Not Speak Its Name

I felt it before we saw anything. It certainly wasn't as enormous as the storm, but it was huge and was abuzz with life I could sense. It was like being in the presence of a whale who was the size of a city. No living thing should be so enormous, but the city was just that. I rubbed my forehead. "What *is* this?" I whispered.

"What?" DNA said, his eyes still closed.

"I think we're getting close."

He looked at me for a long moment. "The Hour Glass is surrounded by a firewall. The Red Eye isn't the only way it stays hidden. I hope it doesn't do to you what the firewall around my village did. It's much bigger and stronger." He looked at the GPS and frowned. I looked too and groaned. The hour was almost up. We had three minutes before the Hour Glass became undetectable to our GPS.

"I hate to say it, AO, but you might be the only way we can find it."

"I'm not even sure I want to find it anyway," I said. "What if they don't want us? What if they know who we are and they think we'll just bring trouble?"

We stared at each other. Where else could we go? If we turned around and went back, it wouldn't be robots and drones waiting for us, it would be human government soldiers. We'd just escaped execution; I just wanted to flee.

"What is it you feel?" he asked.

"Drums," I said.

"You hear drumbeats?"

"Sort of. I hear them, but also feel them. Like the beat is trying to smash my brains. And there's pressure, too." I suddenly wanted to stop the truck, but one look out the window and I was reminded of where we were and what awaited us on the way back. I let the truck keep going and the clock kept counting down. "My brother used to play the drums. They gather people."

Three minutes, the drum beat its rhythm.

Two minutes, the sound bloomed and I could no longer hear the howl of the window outside.

One minute, oh the pressure, and what was I seeing when I closed my eyes? I could not open my eyes.

"It's gone," I heard DNA say.

"I know," I whispered. My ears were blocked with pressure, the pounding in my head was so loud that I wasn't sure if DNA could hear me. But I was seeing things behind my eyes. There was chaos outside and chaos inside my head. Yes, like when I'd arrived at DNA's village. The sensation was so overwhelming that I decided to just fall into it. *Let it take me*, I thought. *Anything was better than this. If I die, I finally die.*

One moment, I was there with DNA, sensing his worry and helplessness, the next, I was swept into blackness. I was falling, though I had no body. I was warm, as if I were falling into something alive. But I had no body. I was not my body. I was . . .

And there were the eyes. Red. So much like the inside of a pomegranate. I don't know when it happened. I began the process long ago. Maybe it started the day I murdered those men. I don't know. I don't know anything. But I knew everything in that moment. And I knew it before them all. I laughed. I had no body but I laughed.

When I opened my eyes, I tasted blood. And blood was running down my nose. I felt it dribbling from my ears. My head was on DNA's lap and he was using his shirt to dab at my wet ears as he wept and said my name over and over, "AO, AO, AO, AO." I lay there for a bit listening to him, my eyes itchy with sweat, my head still pounding, my body aching. His voice was bringing me back. "AO, AO, AO, AO."

We'd stopped because the GPS no longer had a destination. The wind shook the truck and the steer in the back whined with fear, crowding to the front, trying to be as close to DNA as possible.

"I'm okay," I croaked. I coughed, clearing my throat. "I'm okay."

"Are you?"

"I know where the Hour Glass is," I whispered. "Half mile . . ." I paused, reaching out. They answered. "North. There is an entrance. The anti-aejej is like an enormous infinity-shaped dome. It goes pretty high. People have space." I sat up and my head felt like gravity was trying to pull it to the truck's floor. When I shook it, the pounding deepened, so I stopped.

"How do . . . ?" DNA asked.

"I can see it," I said. *Can shut it all down, if I want to?* I wondered. *They will listen to me.* I didn't want to talk about it with DNA or anyone. I wanted to just sit in silence and consider the question of "What am I what am I what am I?" Because WHAT WAS I? I could see it. The Hour Glass existed because an insanely powerful anti-aejej was pushing the storm back so that the hidden desert city of Hour Glass could exist. And on top of that, there was a digital cloaking firewall up that prevented any type of surveillance. Well, unless it was me.

I was seeing, touching, communicating, *controlling*.

I could CONTROL.

I sniffed and tasted more blood. Was my *brain* bleeding? What was all this costing me? But I felt so much better. I touched the screen. I didn't even have to know how to operate it. I told it how to operate and, as I did, I could see that infinite pomegranate of eyes shift to focus more closely on me. A steering wheel template popped up on the touch screen and my seat lowered so that I was eye to eye with it. I put my palms on the screen as the truck began to move again.

"Allah is great," DNA muttered.

I just shook my head. "I'll never ever be able to explain," I said.

We were picking up speed. In the back, GPS mooed loudly as the truck was buffeted by the winds. "I agree," DNA said. "But it could be worse."

"There's going to be an archway," I said. I'd closed my eyes and I could see it. But only because that archway was threaded with surveillance cameras. "I can see us coming. Hour Glass security can, too."

The archway was made of heavy red crystal. Digitally, I could touch it, smell it, search its history. This archway was all that was left of a film set for an old Nollywood movie made by a Nigerian billionaire with little creative vision and lots of time. A movie buff, he'd been determined to make a movie that was greater than Star Wars. He'd insisted on writing the script, directing and even acting in it. Then he'd distributed his cinematic creation all over Africa. The film had been so terrible that to this day it was still known throughout the continent as the "Worst African Movie Ever Made." And this solid rhodochrosite crystal archway that the billionaire had demanded be constructed was all that was left of the film's elaborate africanfuturist set.

All this I could pull instantly from the Internet right in my mind, as I looked at our truck approaching. "There are people guarding it. It's the only way in . . . and out because of the anti-aejej. If you try to go out anywhere else, the velocity of the wind repelling from the anti-aejej will tear you apart. It's actually kind of genius."

"And dangerous," he said. "I don't like places with only one exit."

"Good point," I said. *I could always shut it off,* I thought. *I really could. Maybe. And destroy the Hour Glass in the process. And maybe myself, too.* "But let's go in," I said. "If we have to get out, we'll get out. We'll find a way. We just escaped an execution, getting out of the Hour Glass can't be much harder."

I slowed us to a stop and as if by my command, white flood lights lit up the darkness, showing the swirling dust storm retreating and lifting. And there was the red crystal archway. This close to it, I could see the famous etchings, from Nsibidi to Vah to Adinkra.

"Allah is here," DNA whispered.

"Someone definitely was," I muttered.

All around us was quiet and still. We were in the field of the Hour Glass's giant anti-aejej, but this part of it was like the entrance. In the back of the jeep, GPS mooed softly and the quiet was so profound, I could hear the worry in his voice.

"We're here," I said. "They're going to send . . ."

Ding. It appeared on the screen in bright yellow words.

"How'd you know they were sending that?" DNA asked. "Just curious."

"I can even hear them typing the message," I said. I chuckled.

The message was five words, "Step out of the truck."

"Can they turn their anti-aejej off?" DNA asked.

"Maybe," I said. "We're just past the borders of it. But if

they move the border, I'm sure I can move it back." I really *was* sure. I just wasn't sure if I could do it before the Red Eye's violent winds swept us away or if doing something big like this would hurt me. The thing that had shifted or ruptured in my brain—what if flexing or pushing that something damaged my brain? Maybe I could drop dead at any moment, from a brain aneurism, a heart attack, or stroke if I attempted the wrong thing.

Another message came on the screen. This time it was six words. "Get out of the truck NOW."

"Or what?" I muttered. But we'd come here for a reason. We wanted in. I turned to DNA, "Come on. Let's go."

DNA didn't wait for me to ask again. I opened my door and got out on my side. I carefully took my mask off. The first thing I noticed was that air was free of dust and it was warm, the anti-aejej removing every speck of sand and dust in the air. The Hour Glass would not have dust problems as most places in the desert did. And the quiet was amazing, despite the storm that roiled and raged about a half mile behind and hundreds of feet above us. Beyond the archway, although it was through a veil of whipping dust, I could see the Hour Glass: buildings of stone, giant tents made of fortified weather-treated polymers, glimpses of outdoor camps, and knots of markets. More lights, so many lights, because the storm kept so much of the sunshine from coming through. A refugee city in the shadows.

I walked in front of the truck where DNA met me, followed by GPS and Carpe Diem. We stood facing the archway.

"Wait," DNA said, taking his mask off. Then he shut his eyes.

I nodded. We had to wait anyway, but I knew what he was doing, and it was damn important, in my opinion. I hadn't forgotten what he told me when we first met. How before he and his people had gone into that town, he'd paused. Of all of them, he'd paused. And he'd done what his mother had taught him to do and it had saved his life. Now he was doing it again. Grounding.

I looked down at my metal feet. Was it even possible for *me* to ground? Could the energy of the Earth, the aura of the Hour Glass, travel through the bottoms of my cybernetic feet, into my flesh, all the way to my brain, centering and informing me? I didn't think so.

DNA grunted and looked at me.

"Okay?" I asked.

"We'll see." DNA muttered. "What now?"

"We wait some more," I said.

He nodded, looking ahead at the arch. "No problem."

For over a minute, there was nothing, and the silence was amazing. No wind, no grains of sand tumbling, not even the sound of the city just beyond the archway. We were in a type of sound-proof bubble. Then, "AO and DNA." The voice was female, loud and strikingly clear, and it spoke in Igbo.

We looked at each other yet again. "Do you speak Igbo?" I asked him.

"No," he said.

"That is us," I replied in Igbo. No point in trying to hide who we were. These days, privacy was a myth and there clearly was no secrecy when entering the Hour Glass, anyway. "But DNA doesn't speak Igbo."

"You're on the run, both of you," the voice continued in Igbo. "AO, you're responsible for publicly murdering five men in a market."

"That's an overly simplified way to put it," I said in Igbo.

"We've all seen the footage. We know it was complicated." The voice switched to English. "DNA, you were involved in the incident in Matazu that led to the deaths of seven people and seventy six steer."

DNA shook his head, raising his hands. "I was there. I was involved, but not—"

"We've seen the complete footage," the voice said.

We were both silent. This wasn't our decision to make.

"You've come here to hide," the voice said. "Most people do." There was a long pause and GPS mooed loudly. Carpe Diem grunted at him as if to say, "Shush!" DNA patted her side.

"You're both legends here. We're *proud* to have you."

I saw nothing shift, but I felt it and we both heard it. PHOOOWOOOOOOSH! The veil of dust dissipated and then the sound of vehicles, voices, generators, music, laughter, reached our ears. The sounds of the Hour Glass. The voice spoke again, "Every hour at 1:11, all clocks reset to 12:11, all satellite locations and communication, all passwords reset, as well. We call that The Rotation of the Glass. We live within the chaos. Welcome to the Hour Glass."

DNA and I herded the steer into the back of the truck again. When we got inside, there was another message on the screen for us. "The Force wants to see you. All remote navigation?"

"The Force?" I asked. "What is that? Some Star Wars reference?"

"Does it matter?" DNA asked.

"I don't like the idea of . . ."

DNA reached forward and touched the "OK" button. I frowned but that was that. He was starting to know me. We entered the Hour Glass.

CHAPTER 15

The Force

As we passed through the archway, my head began to ache so much that I couldn't filter it out. Conversations, clicks, flashes of light in my peripheral vision, pinprick feelings in the parts of me that were organic flesh. I didn't mention any of it to DNA. Why ruin the moment for him. Or for me.

First we passed a group of people standing on the sides of the dirt path we drove on. People wearing things from traditional loose garments of the north, to burkas, to jeans and t-shirts and miniskirts and tube tops. I saw dark brown faces, many ages, all watching with curiosity as we slowly passed. People held up cell phones and were taking photos, most were looking with their own eyes and laughing?

Messages started appearing on the screen in the truck.

"Welcome!"

"Righteous murderers!"

"We're glad to have you!"

"Save the cows!"

Some sent links to our truck, email addresses, physical addresses, invitations to meetings, parties, and many sent "clean cash," untrackable 48-hour credits that could be used anywhere without revealing one's identity or even location.

"This is crazy!" I shouted.

DNA laughed, "We're famous."

"Infamous," I said.

"No, the Hour Glass is the greatest refuge from . . ." He
pointed behind us. "All that and beyond. These are the people
who fall through or don't fit. If they've seen the un-doctored
footage, then they have full context."

DNA opened his window as we passed. "Thank you all!" he
shouted. An old woman in jeans and a colorful Ankara top and
giant gold earrings, waved and came forward, "We all know
when that time comes," she said. DNA held out a hand and she
took it. She looked in at me and pointed at me with her other
hand. "You, don't feel badly and don't let insecurity blind you."

"Okay," I said, frowning.

Someone banged at the back of our truck.

"Hey!" DNA shouted turning around.

"Open the back door," another woman said.

DNA got up and went to the back, joining GPS and Carpe
Diem.

"Who is it?" I asked.

"Uh, yeah, open the backdoor," he said. "I think it's okay."

"You *think*?" I asked. He was looking outside the back windows, GPS and Carpe Diem crowding and nuzzling him.

"Just open it."

A giant bale of hay was dumped into the truck a moment
after I did and the steer set upon it immediately. "Thank you,"
DNA said to two women who stood side by side grinning.

"We've been following the chase on the feeds. When we
heard you were here, we knew they'd be hungry," one of the
women said.

The other raised a fist and said, "Let the cows live!"

I raised a fist in solidarity, laughing. DNA shut the door
and came back to the front and we got moving again, more
messages still popping up on the truck's screen. We drove on
the sand path leading into the city, and we were both quiet as

we took it all in. On both sides were a series of stone domes, each with thick poles extending so high that one could barely see what was at the top. But you could *hear* it—large wind turbines, their wide blades slicing the air so fast that they were a blur. They must have extended through the anti-aejej's field.

The stone domes had hundreds of antennae sticking out, making them look like pin cushions. Even as we passed, we saw a group of laughing teens open a stone door to go inside one of the domes. Each of these buildings made my new senses vibrate with their digital connectivity. Along with being enormous sources of electricity, they were each some kind of communication node.

Once we passed these buildings, there was more open space, farms that grew what looked like corn, onions, soybeans, and tomatoes. Huge sunshine lamps flooded the area with so much light, it was as if the sun had risen. "Wow," I said. "It even feels a bit humid here."

"Engineers, scientists, journalists, farmers, lawyers, doctors, even billionaires, there's a *lot* of brain power in the Hour Glass," DNA said. "Every kind of person has a reason to flee here, if they have the guts."

"And if they don't mind never seeing the real sun," I added. "It's like living on the Mars colony. Except it's right here on Earth."

We drove on the dirt road for what seemed like miles. There were markets, the occasional stone building, but it was mostly farmland. People walked along the road. It was peaceful. We arrived at one of the open spaces and a message told us to "get out of the truck, leave the steer, they will be cared for, start walking," so we did. Water was drawn from a network of deep wells in the area and people lived around these wells. What fascinated me most was that, because the anti-aejej prevented rain and wind, people lived right out in the open, not a house in sight. And there was so much open space, privacy wasn't an issue. The sky that people were used to was the maelstrom churning above. There were wide oriental rugs spread over the soft sand in the home areas. People walked about without shoes.

White stone hearths were set up in designated places, and there were wooden tables beside them. Women and sometimes men, crowded around many of these, plates of food, cooked and uncooked on the tables. One man was grilling what looked and smelled like chicken kabobs and ears of corn. A woman stirred something in a giant metal pot. The air in the cooking area we passed smelled of curry, red stew, thyme, wood smoke, stockfish, boiling rice, and incense. The place we walked through reminded me of DNA's nomad village, though it wasn't nomadic at all. These were places and people who did not move.

"Anwuli! What the FUCK!"

Hearing my birth name made me jump. I turned to see a tall, very lean, dark-skinned man wearing a long white kaftan with an intricately embroidered blue collar. For several moments, my mouth hung open. "Oh my God! Force Ogunleye?" I strode over to him. "Are you . . . how . . . what?!!"

Along with the headache and other sensations I was enduring all over my body, the additional shock made me dizzy. It was just too much. Force Ogunleye and I had dated for two years while I was in my teens. We met in auto shop class and bonded immediately over our love of the class materials that most were only there to memorize and then use to make money. Force was the one who'd put in my hands the very first anti-aejej I'd ever held. At the time, he was obsessed with them and I was wondering what the point of them could be. Who needed something that created a protective electromagnetic dome around you during a sand storm?

I was pretty self-centered back then. Completely paralyzed from my upper thighs and down, I was still trying to figure myself out. And I was months away from deciding to have my useless legs removed to allow for cybernetic ones. Most of the time I wasn't dealing with my situation well. I was angry and frustrated and yet to understand that screaming, "It's not fair!" at every problem, machine, and person around made absolutely no difference. Force was always able to distract my rage with ideas and by giving me things to work on with my new cybernetic hand. He was the one who taught me how to use them and that a mechanic with an arm and legs like mine was a superior mechanic.

Force wasn't my first kiss, but he was my first love. Then when he was eighteen, he was called back to his land in the west to be king. He was next in line in one of the lesser Yoruba monarchies. I remember the pressure he was always under. He was constantly told that nothing he loved doing mattered, and if he were ever called to take his position as king, he *had* to do it. It was the only time I'd ever heard him say, "It's not fair." He'd whispered it, but he said it.

"I left," he said now as he hugged me tightly. He let go and looked me over. "But I didn't return to my homeland in Ondo State."

"You came here?"

"Eventually."

We stood staring at each other. I could almost feel DNA's struggle between waiting and demanding he be introduced.

"Why didn't you *tell* me?" I asked. I gazed at his face, feeling tears sting the corners of my eyes. For over a decade, I'd wanted to ask this question to his face.

"I don't like . . ."

"Doesn't matter if you don't like goodbyes," I snapped.

"You ghosted." My heart was throbbing hard now, but I resisted the powerful urge to rub my temples. I didn't want him to see weakness in me right now. He'd ask me if I was okay and shift the focus to my health, my strange body. He used to do this often when we were teens.

"There was a lot," he said. "But I ran from my family, and I didn't want them to track me. So, yes, I ghosted . . . I ghosted everyone." He pressed his lips together and looked down. "I'm sorry."

"Your parents told me you committed suicide!" I shouted. This time I did rub my temples.

"Hello," DNA said, stepping up. "My full name is deoxyribonucleic acid, DNA for short." Force turned to DNA and just stared at him, all the emotion on his face turned toward DNA. I thought he was going to punch DNA in the face.

"Hi," Force said.

———————

I slept for twelve hours. I knew the exact time because I checked with my mind. The ability was still there. I'd slept, though, without being aware that I was being watched and without being aware enough to watch back. I awoke with blood crusting my nose and my left ear. I stared up at the "sky" of chaos for nearly ten minutes. "The Red Eye never closes," I whispered. Swirls and gusts of dust and debris dimly lit by glimpses of sunshine that somehow managed to penetrate the storm. What a "sunrise" it was to look at. I squinted.

What was that? I could have sworn I'd seen a speck of something that wasn't dull sandy brown. It was a glint of something lighter than the shadowy beige of the dust, but I'd only glimpsed it for a second. The ceiling of the anti-aejej's field was about a hundred and fifty feet. High enough for me to not see it clearly, but low enough for me to know I'd seen it.

I shuddered and sat up, looking away from the "sky." I brought my metal legs to my chest and pressed my face to them. The cloth of the long green kaftan spanning my legs was soft and smelled like Force. I inhaled the scent trying to let my angry memories of him overpower the thing I knew I'd seen fly by above. I was still angry with Force but this didn't work. "You know you saw it, you know you saw it," I muttered, pressing my face harder against my legs. "Shit."

I'd just glimpsed one of the most disturbing facts everyone knew about the Red Eye. I'd always assumed it was urban legend designed to keep people away. But I know what I saw. Even if it was for a split second, I know that I saw a cluster of bones. Human bones. When one got caught in the winds of the Red Eye, the winds took you. First the storm thrashed you about until you were dead, then it stripped you of flesh and sinew. And then you flew forever.

The Red Eye's winds were full of the dried tired bones of unlucky people who'd never find rest. Around and around they flew, the winds keeping the bones in their own clusters. I pressed my face to my legs and shut my eyes. Then I opened them because the pomegranate of eyes was looking back at me, and in looking at them, I felt the connection to everything else and this threatened to swallow me. I felt blood oozing into my nose as I took deep breaths to calm myself.

Something lightly kicked one of my metal feet. When I looked up, a young woman was grinning down at me. She was wearing a bright orange sari, no shoes, and her long braids were piled atop her head. "DNA is up already and went for a walk. We all thought you should sleep, but the sun's been out for hours now. The day is going. You want some breakfast?"

I sniffed the blood back into my nose. "I . . . I . . . ugh." I rubbed my head and hair and sighed, getting up. Dolapo was Force's long-time girlfriend. I liked her. Her happy demeanor was its own sunshine, and I needed all the sunshine I could get. She was a coder who'd come to the Hour Glass out of pure curiosity and loved what she discovered so much she decided to stay. She also seemed to be my biggest fan, which was weird.

"I made some egusi soup, dodo, suya, or if you only want a snack, I have dates and groundnuts."

"Thanks, Dolapo, but I'm not hungry."

"Well, just tell me when you're ready. I think you should eat, though. You need your strength." She paused, staring at me with a grin on her face. "Anything you need. I'm over at the hearth for now." Then she bustled off. I dragged myself up and, as I did, I saw Force emerge from between the field of high corn directly behind our sleeping area.

"Dolapo texted me you're finally up," he said.

"Yeah," I said.

"Eat and get dressed, I want to show you something before your DNA returns."

CHAPTER 16

Stone Hut

"What is that?" I asked. It was a soft but steady buzz that started the moment we stepped up to the building. We'd stepped into some sort of gentle electrical field, a feeling I was actually quite used to with all my cybernetic parts.

"You're being scanned," Force said. "I know, it feels weird. Some feel it more than others, but everyone feels it. It's why we call them Mosquito Huts. They buzz in your ear and take a bit of your blood."

"Ah, my 'blood' being my information."

"Yep." He had to really put his shoulder into shoving the heavy door open. I probably should have helped him. It was solid stone. And when it opened, warm air wafted out like the breath of a beast.

"They made these structures like apocalyptic fortresses in case there's ever an anti-aejej outage," he said.

I blinked, stepping in after him. "Oh goodness! Has that ever happened here?"

Inside the concrete hut was more concrete, except for the tree-trunk thick steel pole that ran through and out and up into the sky. It was surrounded by a chunky concrete spiral stair case.

"Yes, some years ago. I wasn't here for it, thank goodness. There was some sort of breach. To this day no one knows who or what it was. I'll always suspect Ultimate Corp because the

Hour Glass had ended its business in this region not long before."

"You mean The Reckoning? The outage happened right after that happened?"

He nodded.

"So what happened when the anti-aejej went off?"

He chuckled as we ascended the staircase. "What do you
think? Deadly chaos. Thankfully there was about a minute
warning, so most could get their asses inside, or switch on
their own personal antis, but my God, so many were lost to the
winds that day. Men, women, children. It's the risk we all take
living here."

I followed him closely as we went up the stairs. "A risk
worth taking?"

"Definitely."

I gasped when I entered the room that was the small top
floor of the hut. "But on the outside this place is . . ." I sighed
and just stared. It wasn't even like looking through windows. It
was as if we'd stepped outside. I could see across the city, I
could look up into the darkening turbulent sky. "I don't understand."

"You're looking at screens," he said.

I stepped up to what looked like the edge of the roof. My
feet touched a barrier, but my eyes couldn't tell that it was a
screen. I reached out and pressed my fingertips to it. It was
warm.

"And only the inside of *this* power hut has all these crazy
screens It's the Hour Glass's main hub," he said. "I not only
built this, I run it. With a team, of course."

"Really?"

"Yes. My skills have improved since we last talked."

"Did you build the programming that resets and protects the Hour Glass, too?"

"Hell no," he said, laughing hard. "That was built by Maiduguri, the low level AI who still runs this place. Maiduguri was created by one of the first groups to come here." He sat on the well-worn couch in the center of the room. "Sit, AO."

I walked around the room first. Touching the screen, marveling at its realism up close, thinking and ignoring the pounding in my ears and neck. In the back of my mind, I could see the pomegranate of eyes. This room was live with wifi. I sat beside him, staring at the pigeon sitting on the edge of the hut. So wildlife, at least the kind often referred to as "rats with wings," lived in the Hour Glass, too. Had they been introduced here, or were they, too, refugees?

"What?"

He looked at me, and I looked at his face up close. I'd analyzed every detail of this face years ago when I couldn't move, when I was in so much pain, when I didn't know what I was or could be. His full lips with the delicate crease in the middle, his high cheekbones that showed off the power of his bloodline, and the brown spot in the white of his left eye, all had given me comfort. He looked the same, just older and more him.

"What did they do to you?" he asked.

I smiled and shook my head. "*I* did this to me," I said. "It was all my choice."

"Being born crippled and then being mangled by a damn car?"

"The part after all that," I snapped.

"You have a twisted idea of what choice is," he said. "My choice was dropping my whole life to be king of some small kingdom or being disowned."

I wiped my face with my hands and groaned. I knew what he was asking. "I don't know, Force."

"Well, tell me about it, then."

"I just said I don't know."

"You know. I know you."

"You don't know me anymore," I said.

"Men attacked you in your local market while you were shopping and you killed them all with your bare hands in front of thirty-one people. Oh I definitely still know you."

"I don't know exactly what happened," I said. "I'm not a murderer. Those men would have killed me."

"I know." He paused. "I watched it several times, closely. But what *happened* to you?"

DNA and the steer were back at Force's outdoor home. For the moment, we were all safe. It was time to face what I didn't want to face. I groaned again, and even then I knew that *they* heard. "They always hear now," I said, curling over myself. I pressed my face to my hard knees. I curled my arms around myself. And I wailed. For the first time, I accepted it, opened myself to it. I wailed into my knees until my lungs burned, my organic intestines turned, my human heart beat so hard that I felt dizzy. When I opened my eyes, everything was blurred.

Force's hands were on my shoulders, gently pressing me down. "Shhhh, AO, shhhh, calm down." He sat back and reached for something on the floor. Then I felt him reach into my shirt. "Don't move," he said. I trusted him enough to not tear his head off. "Sit back. Breathe. If I think what's happening is happening, your life depends on it. Breathe. Deep breaths."

I could feel my heart slamming in my chest, everything was crowding me, I opened my mouth wide. "Inhale," I heard him say. "Like you are the Red Eye itself!" I inhaled. "Your blood pressure is class three," he muttered. "Calm yourself."

I breathed. My mouth wide. I imagined the chaos of the Red
Eye. Wind moving in every direction. Suctioning my thoughts
like one of its many whirlwinds. Whooooooooooooooooo. Then
I exhaled a storm. Haaaaaaaaaaaaa.

"That's it, my love, that's it," I heard him say. I could hear
his fingers tapping. When I opened my eyes, I saw that he was
typing on a large tablet. The beat of my heart simulated on its
screen, along with my blood pressure and other diagnostics. At
least ten minutes had passed because he said, " I analyzed that
footage of what happened in that Abuja market. You coughed,
like in that moment, you had a hard time breathing."

I shook my head. "I don't remember."

"I just put a diagnostic tab on your chest," he said. "And
now I see that what I suspected was correct." He put up a hand.
"Relax, you're better now. Don't let this, uh, surprise you too
much but your blood pressure is just shy of a full on heart attack. But you're better now, you're better now."

Heart attack, I thought. "Is that why I feel my pulse so
strongly in my ears?" He nodded. "And the headaches," I said.
"Like a drum beat." When was the last time I had my blood
pressure checked? Or maybe it got bad when I killed those
men. I kissed my teeth. What did it matter? "I think . . . I can
talk to them."

"Talk to who?"

"The AI. All of them. Around the world, in space, all the
programs, software. Even the Hour Glass's AI Maiduguri." I
paused. "And I think I can make them do what I *want*."

He didn't believe me. Even after I told him how DNA and I
escaped the warehouse, Force chose to believe his theories and
logical scientific explanations, instead. He said it was all just
my high blood pressure and coincidence. The high blood pressure and stress interfered with my perception of what was

happening around me. In the meantime, the corporation decided that a public execution of someone as damaged as me
was bad press. He was sure that the Nigerian government may
have done something to me, and they'd ordered the corporation to back off so they could retrieve their specimen.

Anything but me being a living wireless connection, simultaneously human and machine; the result of an abnormal
amount of flesh to machine wiring, some random glitch caused
by the combination of violence inflicted on my body, and sub-
sequent rage.

"It's been too much for you," he said still looking at his
tablet. "All of it. Years of it. The surgeries, the artificial parts,
what comes with all that. Look at these numbers. Your heart is
still flesh, it *can* die."

"I don't CARE." We were quiet for a moment. I felt better
now. I took more deep breaths. Those definitely helped. Steady
even breaths. I took a bit more time. Then I went in . . .

Dusty dirt roads . . .

Some paved with fresh black asphalt, but mostly dusty . . .

Few cars, even fewer autonomous vehicles. It was locating
the small Ondo state town I still remembered that led me to
the building I sought. The mosque didn't look like a mosque
and the church across the street looked like someone's modest
home. There was a small shop down the road from the mosque
where you could still buy goods like chewing gum, incense
sticks, and cigarettes with actual cash. And Force's family's palace was right beside the mosque.

All this I showed Force on the screens around us that were
normally used for lectures, surveillance, and programming.
Screens that Force had control of and that I, according to him,
didn't. "I still remember the name of your town. That's why I
can show it to you. I tell them the name and they find the

satellite images. What I'm showing you is your town a few years ago. When I thought you had committed suicide and your family told me they didn't want me at your funeral because your death was *my* fault."

"They told you that?"

"Yes." I opened my eyes and glared at him. All around us was Ikare, Ondo State, Nigeria. There was the palace where Force was born, where he had apparently never gone when I thought he had. I made the images move a bit as if we were walking on foot through his home. I watched him as I did this, it was that easy. The Control. "I'm doing all this. I ask and they obey me, indulge me, whatever."

"Okay," he said, a blank look of shock on his face. "So who is obeying or indulging you? Who is 'they'?"

"They're a sentience, the Internet? No more than that. They're digital and ubiquitous. In my mind, they look like eyes, fruit, a pomegranate." I glanced at him and then quickly glanced away, not liking how he was looking at me. I shook my head. "I can't explain." I switched the image to my face, as if I were looking at him from all around, five of my faces from the various angles of the cameras in the room, looking at him. I could feel the drums in my temples, and I took a deep breath. "Whether you believe me or not, I can do this," I said.

"Okay," he said again. "Stop, for now. Your heart rate is increasing."

I stopped and sat back, breathing deeply.

"How?" he asked.

"I don't know."

"It's easy?"

"Minus the risk of heart attack, yes."

"What about your herdsman friend, DNA? Is he involved?"

"*That* part is strange coincidence."

He shook his head. "No."

I shrugged.

"Unfortunately, I don't think you're safe here," he said.

"I'm not safe anywhere."

"Yes," he said. "But if what you tell me is true, if you can do this . . . this thing, they're going to want you."

"Who? The government? I'm not . . ."

"No, *Ultimate Corp*. And you should fear them *more* than the government."

"I'll know when they all are coming."

"Maybe, maybe not. Even if you can control all AI, all software, you're still human. You can't be everywhere at once, talking to everyone at once, preparing for everything at once. When you look one way, they'll come at you another."

I frowned. "Maybe."

"There's something else," he said. He sighed. "How's your mother?"

I chuckled. "Fine. My mom and my dad, well, as fine as they could be knowing all that's going on."

"Your mother loved olives," he said. "I remember that."

I laughed. "Of course *you'd* know that. What about it?"

Force and my mother had always had an interesting rapport, which made his leaving all the more profound. They simply enjoyed sitting and talking. Some days, when I was in my worst pain, unable to talk, Force would come over, and he and my mother would sit and just talk. Listening to them made me feel better, though it also made me feel left out.

"I know too much," he said, looking away. He got up and walked to the edge of the room. When he turned back to me, I felt ill.

"What?" I asked. "What is it?"

"You really don't know, do you?"

I frowned more deeply. "Know what?"

"Olives."

"What about olives?" I snapped.

"Ultimate Corp sold almost all the olives in Nigeria, they still do. Some two decades ago, there was a small batch of Beldi olives that they grew in Morocco. I never told you, but I researched this when we were sixteen. Those trees were genetically modified to grow in higher density *and* with a spicy black-peppery taste. They were wildly popular here, you put them in jollof rice, Indomie, ate them as a snack. Unfortunately, these olives were later proven to cause birth defects if one ate too many of them. They recalled all those Beldi olives, it was big news. For about a day. Then it wasn't. What never made the news was that five pregnant women in Nigeria ate too many." He paused, and when I just stared at him, he continued. "There were five born like you. Two died days later, though I'm not really sure if their deaths were natural, if you know what I mean."

"I know what you mean," I whispered. They'd most likely been euthanized. Probably with their parents' consent. The only alternative was having a "demon" child.

"Aside from you, two had parents who agreed to a few cybernetic organs. But those parents were Christian Pentecostals, so their religious and cultural beliefs made them reject the most important ones. So one of them died around the age of two and the one who survived, aside from you, remains the . . ." he took a deep breath.

"Say it," I said.

"Shameful family secret," he said after a moment.

"Still alive?"

"If you want to call that life," he said. "So you were the only one who chose to walk *into* the fire. They could *never* get *anyone* to volunteer for what you've been through—"

"I'm an experiment," I blurted.

He looked sad as he said it. "Yes. And they can say you volunteered for it."

"Fuck!" I screamed. I frowned, calming myself. "So . . . so, they *knew* pregnant women would eat those fucking olives? They *wanted* them to?! To cause mutations in their unborn children? So . . . so. . . . they made me *need* all my augmentations?! *Then* they gave me access to it, and then they monitored me?"

"Definitely."

"Okay," I said. Full capacity. A shiver flew from my feet to the top of my head. I opened my mouth to catch my breath. "Stop!" I screamed. Thump, thump, thump, in my ears.

"I researched it all," he whispered. "Found solid answers."

I inhaled deeply, concentrating on my heartbeat, trying to dodge the realization that was slipping into my consciousness no matter how I tried to keep it out. I managed to slow my heart's rhythm, but I couldn't keep out the information Force had just dumped on me. "Because of olives," I said, my eyes closed, my fingertips pressed to my temples.

"She still had one of the jars."

"She kept it? All these years?" I asked.

He nodded.

"So she knew," I said. "She must have researched, too."

"Or they'd visited your home when you were born, and your parents never told you."

So Ultimate Corp was responsible for me being born as I was. Then the government was responsible for enthusiastically giving me whatever augmentation I requested. I thought about the car accident years later. An autonomous vehicle. An accident that the news feeds and engineers said had never happened before. That was so rare it was anomalous. An accident that shouldn't have happened. Maybe that was them pushing me further, to see what more they could do. They must have been delighted every time I petitioned for something. I'd made their job easy. No wonder my petitions were always accepted. I'd thought I was just lucky, applying at the right time, stating my need in the right way. "Shit," I said.

"Yeah. Shit."

I couldn't keep the tears from dribbling from my eyes. I wiped them away with the back of my flesh hand. Thump thump thump, the beat of my brother's drums in my ears. I saw flashes of what I did to those men. And then my vision blurred as, for the first time, I *remembered* in full. I'd crushed the beautiful man's throat with my cybernetic hand as I looked him in the face. The sound and feeling of it echoed in my mind. And once the memory was there, it didn't leave this time. It stayed. It stayed. Oh it stayed. "God," I muttered, barring my teeth, clenching my fist. Thump, thump, thump. I welcomed it.

I got up and walked to the screen. I was now taking us through a dense jungle. I stopped and stared at it. I liked this place. It was like being able to see what was on my mind as it was on my mind. "They'll kill us both, eventually."

"Not if you kill them first."

I laughed.

"I'm serious, Anwuli. Maybe it's time you stopped running. Turn and face your pursuers. Just think about it." He got up. "They won't find you any time soon. The Hour Glass is still the Hour Glass. You're definitely the most valuable person to come through here, but you aren't the most dangerous."

"I find that oddly comforting."

"Heh, that's why few people who come to live in the Hour Glass ever leave."

A black box opened in the center of the screen. Inside it, in bright red, was 1:10. Then it began counting upwards. Less than a minute until it was 1:11, the Reset, the time when all data in all clouds and networks going out and coming into the Hour Glass was wiped and everything restarted. Sand began to blow across all the screens and it was so realistic looking and sounding, that I actually started feeling wind! I looked at the floor to make sure there was nothing hitting my feet. It increased and soon the image of outside was awash in sand. Everything but the counting clock.

When it reached 1:11, it all went black. Force sat back down on the couch. "Have a seat for a second." As I sat beside him, windows began to open up all over the screens. Three-hundred-sixty degrees of current news. It was so overwhelming that I laughed out loud. All the people speaking, all the images, all the motion, all the urgency, all the emotion, from all over Africa. Now now now. It was so similar to what it was like to close my eyes and reach out, except for one thing; I was looking, seeing, hearing, but no one was looking *back* at me as I did so. And I couldn't interact.

I was in the middle of one of Africa's worst disasters worrying about being hunted down by one of the world's biggest corporations and my own government. Yet, the rest of Africa was going about its business as usual. Elections were being held in Ghana. There were protests for gay rights in Kenya again. The latest Oracle Solar farm, this one in Chad, was now online. There was a new rap group in Algeria taking the world by storm. Drone deliveries in Mali were going so well that this was the fifth month without a single mishap.

We were both quiet as we caught up with the rest of Africa. And that must have been how I saw it. Out of all the hundreds of stories all around me, I saw it. A smaller box. Maybe because the male newscaster was standing in a place so empty, sand dunes behind him. A familiar sight. It caught my eye. ". . . this small nomadic village could never have seen it coming," the newscaster was saying. Without thinking, I brought it forth and expanded it to a size I could see clearly.

As the anchorperson spoke, I zoomed the focus in on those behind him. As I did it, I held up my hands and parted them as if I were opening up a large map. There. "That's DNA's mother," I said. She looked confused and her hair was in disarray, her skin dirty with soot.

"At approximately 2 AM this morning," the anchorperson said, ". . . this village was set upon by their own. It is believed that this is the home village of the fugitive herdsman at large, Dangote Nuhu Adamu. In these remote parts of Nigeria, as we saw from yesterday's failed capture of the herdsman Adamu and the murderess Okwudili, it is difficult for authorities to quell lawlessness. Bukkaru, the United Fulani Tribal Council elders, a godchild of the organization known as Miyetti Allah, authorized this attack. And there were casualties. This small village was razed to the ground. And still, Adamu was not caught . . . ."

Behind the anchorperson, DNA's mother was being hugged by, yes, DNA's journalist brother. He too was dirty with soot. Where was DNA's sister? "DNA will be angry," I muttered.

"I'm sure," Force said. "And this makes three groups that are after you two now."

"Do they ever go after the *actual* terrorists?"

"If Ultimate Corp can pay people off to stop living the way they've been living for hundreds of years to, instead, plant trees in the parts of the north that aren't engulfed in the Red Eye, they can pay off the Bukkaru to go after one of their own."

"We barely escaped them," I said. "My God. What would they have done to us?"

"Necklace you, watch you burn, and then thrown your bones in the Red Eye to fly forever."

I stared at Force, my mouth hanging open.

"I've heard of desert folk doing that to their worst criminals," he said with a shrug. "At least you can rest easy knowing they won't come here. Tribals don't come to the Hour Glass unless they're outcast."

I got up. "I have to tell DNA."

Force raised a hand and all the screens popped away and we were back to being surrounded by the outdoors. "Yeah, let's get back." He paused. "I'm sorry, AO. For both of you. Neither of you deserves this shit."

I looked into his eyes and then turned to the door. "It's all right," I said, my voice husky. If I had looked at him a moment longer, I'd have burst into tears. The days when I leaned on Force were long gone. Still, as we headed down the stairs, my chest was tight with grief. No, neither of us deserved this shit. "When's the last time you saw the sun?" I asked. I needed to change the subject.

"Real or artificial? There are sun dome restaurants and small parks with lights that create sunshine here that looks even more real than the real thing."

"When's the last time you saw the *real* sun?"

"About five years."

I thought about this conversation well into the night.

CHAPTER 17

Milk

When we got back to Force and Dolapo's space, Dolapo had a full spread of dinner waiting for us, and DNA was sitting at the table beside the stone hearth, eating from a plate of groundnuts.

"AO," he said, grinning. "You look much better than you did this morning."

I laughed sitting beside him. "You, too. Where'd you go?"

"Walking," he said. "We're so close to the Hour Glass border; I wanted to see it. People don't like living near the borders, so the walking there was quiet, peaceful."

"What's out there?" I asked.

"Mostly farms," Force said, sitting across from us. He took a groundnut from DNA's plate and popped it into his mouth. "Groundnut farms. I assume you found the path that runs right alongside the anti-aejej edge."

DNA perked up even more. "Yes! I walked it for nearly a mile, and not one person or vehicle passed me. I know why. AO, it's beautiful and quiet, but the storm! You can *see* it. Whirling and swirling. And the higher you look, the thinner the dust gets, so the *more* you see. And you *can't* hear it. So you see how violent it is, but you don't truly know."

"But all of us *do* know because we all fought our way through the damn thing to get here," Force said. "Yep, nothing but human ingenuity is between us and the Great Flying Death."

"I met a groundnut farmer sitting at a small hut he'd built. He was sitting on a stool watching the storm while he was digitally surveying his crops. He said that every day, he would come out there and converse with the Red Eye. He was a little strange. But he gave me this bag of groundnuts. Said he had a surplus and more money than he could ever spend in his lifetime, and if the Red Eye eventually blew this place away, he was fine going with it."

"Ah, that had to be Sokoto," Dolapo said as she put a huge bowl of egusi soup and a plate of pounded yam in front of me. "The man is over 80 years old and one of the few here the day they created the Hour Glass. His younger sister was one of the founders. No one sees much of Sokoto these days. You are blessed."

I went to the faucet beside the hearth and washed my hands, taking more time with my flesh hand than my cybernetic one. When I sat back down in front of my food, I looked at Force. As it had always been with us, I didn't need to say a word. He simply nodded, stood up, wrapped an arm around Dolapo's waist, and the two gave DNA and me some privacy. DNA glanced at me from the corner of his eye, but said nothing as he munched on groundnuts. I paused and then tucked into my egusi soup.

For several minutes, we sat there. DNA eating groundnuts and me eating the most delicious egusi soup I'd ever tasted. My mother's fantastic skills couldn't compete with this because what made this soup so delicious was not in the execution, it was the ingredients. The chicken tasted amazing, tough but flavorful in a way I'd never experienced. The bitter leaf, ground melon seeds, crayfish, onion, everything tasted as if it was in its fullest color, at peak perfection. "Oh my goodness," I said. "The *taste*!"

"All desert grown," DNA said, smirking. "Even the crayfish. Dolapo said there's some guy who has these pools where he grows all kinds of seafood he's modified to grow small and fast. And they're fed on the freshest ingredients. People pre-order months in advance."

I paused, frowning at my food, then kept eating. About halfway through my meal, I stopped, wiped my hands with the napkin Dolapo had left for me, and turned to DNA. He turned to me, too. "What?" he asked.

Startled by his directness, I looked away. "N . . . nothing," I stammered. "I was just—"

"Look, I'm not usually around people this much. That makes me pretty sensitive. And for some reason, I find you really easy to read. What do you want to tell me? Is it about GPS and Carpe Diem? I think they're okay. Those animal rights people are treating them better than any human b—"

"No, no, Your steer are fine. In the best hands they can be in, other than you."

"It's refreshing," he said, looking at his plate of finished groundnuts. "But I miss them and they're all I—"

"DNA, I saw something," I blurted. "It was your village."

I quickly told him all I knew, which was actually a lot more than I let on to Force. It wasn't that I didn't trust Force. Force had lied to me, horribly. But that was a long time ago, and I understood why. I guess. I didn't tell Force because I felt this was information for DNA's ears only. It was *his* family, *his* village.

"There is footage of the council, the Bukkaru, leaving with your sister Wuro. They came to your village, when the elders refused to tell them where you went, words were exchanged. That old man, the blind one—"

"Papa Ori? No."

"Yes, he said something. The recorded conversation posted on Bukkaru networks didn't catch it. But whatever he said, caused such rage that the Bukkaru had your village ransacked under the pretense of looking for you."

"Where is Wuro?" he said. "Can you locate her?"

I shook my head. "They must have seen what I did yesterday. They won't know how I did it, but they are definitely staying offline. There isn't a whisper of her. There's more."

"Go on."

I sighed. "This whole thing has sparked something. The farming communities seem to also have sent out groups of men—no, mobs of men into the desert." I couldn't look him in the eye when I said it. "They're killing the last of the true herdsmen."

"Shit," DNA hissed.

It was the first time I'd ever heard DNA curse. I don't think he even knew he did it.

"I'm sure this pleases Ultimate Corp," he said. "We are a stupid people. We are killing our last source of homegrown fresh meat and milk. We'd rather eat flesh grown in a lab, or even plastic, than true food. Wish I could just leave this planet with my cows and live on the moon." He got up, sat back down, then got up, sat back down. Frowned. Sighed. Kissed his teeth. Looked at me. "What do I do?"

"I don't know."

"This is my fault."

"I don't agree."

He got up and started pacing. "What do I do, what do I do, what did Wuro say? Why my sister?"

"Because they're trying to get to *you.*"

He was pacing faster now. "They burned everything?"

"Almost."

"Where is my family now?"

"I don't know. They've gone into the desert, though. Not into the Red Eye, just away."

"I know where," he said. He stopped, looking off toward the farms. Then he just started walking.

"Wait! Where are you going?" I asked, jumping up. He didn't stop. He walked faster, and I had to jog to catch up with him. He walked onto a path that led between a field of corn and a field of onions.

"Wait! Where—"

"Where is there space?" he said with a shaky voice. "I *need* it. This way, I think." He was practically running now, but I easily kept up. When he finally stopped, we were on a patch of sand where nothing grew. Where no soil was mixed with the sand. Between corn, onion, soybean fields. It wasn't a wide space, just an in-between place before a field of corn began and a field of peri ended. The area in this spot wasn't fortified with soil, so it was the sand of the land. Old. Dry. Barren. Here, he fell to his knees and clutched his head in his hands.

"Geno," he said. "Geno, you extracted the universe from a drop of milk. Milk flowed, even out here in the desert. Please, please *help* me." He dropped into Pulaar and for several minutes, he was completely lost to me. Then suddenly, he stopped his frantic praying, talking, pleading, whatever he was doing. He thrust both his hands deep into the soil and shut his eyes.

I will never believe in Christ or Allah or any other God. I will never follow any religion. Up until three days ago, I did not believe in juju. Not in oracles, charms, or anything that human beings think they can control. My life was an example that there was no such thing as true human control. But I'd been in a sorcerer's hut yesterday, smoking sorcerer's weed. With my mind, I'd stopped machines from executing me,

DNA, and his two remaining steer. And when he buried his hand into the sand, through the sensors on the bottoms of my cybernetic feet, I felt the sand I stood on warm up like a sunrise. I swear it.

"My mother," he said, his eyes still closed. "I saw her do this once. Her youngest brother was one of those who fought the Ultimate Corp security at the warehouse that day. She heard about how it burned and so many were killed. She needed him to come home. So she dug her hands in the dirt and prayed to our Earth to return him. He was covered in soot, but he walked into our compound two minutes later."

I sat beside him and dug my hands in the sand, too. "What are we asking for?"

"Help. To find my sister. Help for my fellow true Fulani herdsman; we're *not* terrorists."

I shut my eyes and did my best. Instead of the Earth, I found myself talking to the pomegranate of eyes. I kept my breathing steady and deep, staying aware of my physical body. Calm. I had to stay calm. *Where is she?* I asked. I cannot describe the feeling but I felt and saw it *all*, despite the fact that my brain was unable to process it. Perspectives, voices, words, screenshots, word searches. We were sweeping. There was a text message. It said, "It's ok. Wuro will sit." The text had a number. We followed it. Triangulated its signal, disregarded where the number was based.

"I know where your sister is," I said, opening my eyes. "West of the Red Eye, near the Nigeria-Niger border."

"That's where the Bukkaru council holds its most important meetings," DNA said. "It's where they know they'll be only amongst themselves. Do you know what they're doing there?"

"The text message said, 'It's ok. Wuro will sit.'"

He frowned, shaking his head. "I don't know what that means. There was no other information?"

"I can dig, but not without alerting them to my presence. Might be better to do that when we have a plan."

"True," he said. "Are you all right?"

I smiled. "I'm fine."

"Good," he said. "So . . . can you do a little something more?"

It didn't take me long to locate them. And because it was simple, finding them didn't hurt me. DNA knew the exact details to give, but he couldn't have known that those he had asked me to seek had arrived in the Hour Glass so recently. I located and sent them messages. Two hours later, they came through the cornfields. We'd waited there and when the corn stalks started rustling, we both thought they were something else.

"Are there wild animals here?" I asked, jumping to my feet.

"Pigeons, lizards, geckos, flies, the occasional scorpion, things like that, nothing big," he said, keeping his eyes on the rustling corn stalks. They came one by one. Within a minute of each other. Three of them. All men. When they emerged from the corn field, they stood staring at each other, surprised to see someone else emerging from the corn. One of them couldn't hold back his tears, and he angrily looked away. The other two held DNA's strong gaze. I took over when it was clear none of them planned to speak.

"Hi," I said. "I'm the one who found you and sent a message. Can you tell me your names?"

"Lubega," the one who was crying said. Tall and thin and

the blue kaftan and jeans he wore made him look even more so. He couldn't have been older than nineteen.

"Tasiri," the one who looked about DNA's age said. Tall with light brown skin, his dreadlocks were so strong that they stood straight up despite being inches long. "Who are you?"

"See them now," the third one said, looking at Lubega and Tasiri. He could have been about thirty-five and was wearing nothing but red shorts. "This is why we came, right? To see them with our own eyes?" He pointed at DNA, glaring. "Do you understand what is happening? What you've done?"

"I didn't do *anything*," DNA snapped. "You know that. You saw the video. And you saw them kill my steer and my friends and *their* steer! I carry no Liquid Sword. I'm no terrorist."

"Idris," I said. He froze and stared at me. "Yeah, I know your name. I know a lot of things. Another thing I know is that I don't have energy for this wahala. You've just been through hell. I understand. But I didn't call you here to unload on DNA. He needs your help. And it'll help you three, too." I paused. "Please. Hear him out." I stepped back.

"Thank you, AO," he said. He turned to the herdsman. "Before I ask, please, I want to hear what happened to you. I need to know the details. How, why, when."

It was surprisingly Idris who told us everything. His English was the strongest.

They'd indeed arrived in the Hour Glass hours ago. There was no one to vouch for them, so a human rights group had stepped forward to offer them temporary housing, food, and care. They'd arrived with wind lacerations having walked all night through the Red Eye with nothing but a personal anti-aejej to protect them. Personal aejejs were too weak to protect a person adequately from the strong winds of the Red Eye, so, although they weren't swept away, they'd been pelted for hours

and hours, miles and miles with the blowing sand that pene-
trated the anti-aejej's protective field.

The five of us sat on the sand in a sort of circle, Lubega and
Tasiri beside Idris, DNA and I across from them.

"We had no choice," Idris said. "The three of us, we meet
every month at a petrified palm tree a mile or so from the Red
Eye. It's a nice place to meet and a reminder that though we are
few, we are still here. Even in these strange times. Our steer
rest, and we sit and gaze at the disaster while we drink milky
tea, eat whatever we have to eat, share stories and updates; then
we part ways in the morning. We go in different directions every time. None of us goes north."

"Until yesterday," Lubega said.

"We was drinking tea," Tasiri said. "I was the one who saw."

"Tasiri had his back to the Red Eye because he hates it,"
Idris said. "That's what saved us. They were far away, maybe
three miles, but Tasiri has a good eye, and he saw them coming, speeding in trucks. They were spread out. They meant to
force us to flee in one direction."

They got up. They got their steer up. Then they herded
them toward the Red Eye, the only direction they could go. For
several minutes they ran toward doom, the vehicles of the Bukkaru and farmer villages easily and quickly closing in on them.
Every so often, they'd shoot into the air to show they were
armed and ready. Idris couldn't speak of what happened next.
Lubega told the rest, his eyes filling with tears. He spoke in
Pulaar and DNA had to translate for me.

The vehicles pursuing them stopped after a certain point
and Idris, Lubega, and Tasiri and all their 125 steer kept running. The steer would follow their humans into a wall of fire
and the Red Eye was no different. And this was how the three
of them got to witness all their steer whisked into flying deaths

by the Red Eye while they stood huddled in the force field of
Lubega's anti-aejej, a gift from his father when he'd left home
to continue the ancient tradition of the herdsman life.

"Why?" DNA asked. "Why you three?"

"It was not just us three," Idris said. "It was all of us. You
see, the same day you left your village, the Bukkaru issued an
order on all herdsmen."

"An order?" DNA shouted. "That fast? No. It hasn't even
been—"

"The only thing that makes sense is that the Bukkaru must
have signed an agreement with the non-Fulani farming communities *weeks* ago. Had it ready," Idris said. "All they needed
was a reason most would support. You gave it to them. Well,
really, it was something one of your village elders said, the one
with the walking stick, if we are being specific."

"Papa Ori," DNA said.

"Yes. The meeting in your village was recorded and it was
all over the village feeds," Idris said. "Your Elders refused to
turn you over. We don't know what it was, but whatever Papa
Ori said to the head of the Bukkaru in your defense, that's what
got your village destroyed and the order executed."

DNA rubbed his face. "So does this mean all the other
herdsmen are dead?"

"All they could find," Idris said. "They tracked most of us
through our interactions on the village feeds, so they found
us fast."

Tasiri muttered something and DNA translated. "He says
he thinks . . ." he sighed. "He thinks we are the only Fulani
herdsmen left. No men with steer roam the north anymore. It's
the end of an era."

"Wiped out *that* fast?" I asked. "It's only been a day since we
left there."

Idris shrugged and then slumped, looking defeated. Tasiri picked at a still raw-looking laceration on his arm. Lubega looked at his hands and shook his head.

"Herdsmen only want peace," DNA muttered. "Everyone who truly *knows* this knows we don't kill anybody."

"The ones terrorizing people are now just area boys," Idris said to AO. "They willingly gave up their heritage because they saw no more value in it. They became like people in the cities, colonized to the point of forgetting. To them everything's worth is measured by money and material things. My brother . . . he is one." He sighed. "He is lazy and has no heart because he wants more than he can get. Before he turned to terrorizing, he tried to work for Ultimate Corp in the south. They wouldn't give him a job because he could not prove his place of birth. My family have no place of birth, we are nomads. So my brother chose the way of the gun."

Again, Ultimate Corp's name coming up when speaking of a recent tragedy. It was the common denominator in all that had happened and was happening. I got up and walked away from them. *Let them have time together,* I thought. *Let them be herdsmen, and let me get away from their misery.* I stopped amongst the onions and inhaled their sweet spicy scent. I don't know why I did it. There could be a thousand reasons and there could be no reason. I went inward and there I asked *them* to find my parents.

"Oh," I whispered, learning something more about what I could do. It was *easy* and it was fast and *there* was my mother in her kitchen, I could see her through her phone. And there was my father outside on the balcony, looking over New Calabar, his favorite place to think. Both were quiet, seemingly at peace, as they always were. I watched them, simultaneously, for I was not watching with my physical eyes. I watched with cameras that were also my eyes, I looked at something else. I watched my father gazing across the city from the high rise they lived in. I watched my mother stir a large pot of okra soup. Then I watched the interview with them on NNN, Nigeria National News.

The story was fed not only nationwide, not only continent-wide, but worldwide. Over ten thousand news sources, including every single major news source in the world. "Oh," I moaned. I was swaying on my feet, but I felt so far from my body in this moment. I watched my parents' interview with NNN. It had gone live earlier today.

They sat in the living room. The very same place I'd sat in my wheelchair when I was healing from my cybernetic leg transplants. On the same couch Force and I had sat on when we'd shared our first kiss. For the interview, my mother had gotten her hair freshly braided in long gray individuals long enough to pool in her lap. My father had shaven his salt and pepper beard and looked ten years younger. He also wore a blue cap that matched his embroidered blue shirt. They looked good.

"That's not my daughter anymore," my father was saying. I'd begun watching in the middle of the interview. Even in my scattered state, I knew not to begin at the beginning. The meat would be in the middle. "Something has destroyed her brain function. We certainly never wanted her to get all those augmentations."

My mother was nodding. My mother who'd birthed my broken body. Then she added, "I don't even know where she was learning about all that. We are good Christians." Her breath caught, but she was able to continue. "What God gives is best. Now see the devil working through her."

My heart was breaking. It's true, my parents had never

wanted me to change myself as much as I had changed myself. I knew they tolerated me more than they embraced me. But to tell the world this was something else entirely. I shouldn't have been so shocked, but I was. I should have stopped watching once I knew they were okay. I should not have skipped ahead to the meat of the interview.

The camera zoomed in on my father as he said, "I pray the government is able to get to her before she hurts more people. But that's not my daughter anymore."

Enough. No. I needed to know one more thing. And there was the information I sought: My brother had not been available for comment. I let go immediately, opening my eyes. I wasn't only crying, my nose was bleeding. I was standing and leaning forward, as if I were about to faint and this saved the blue t-shirt Dolapo had lent me. The blood spattered onto my metal feet. My head thumped, and I stumbled forward. I knelt down, a metal index finger digging into the sand for purchase, flesh fingers pressing my temples.

"Let me just die," I whispered. I sighed. I'd thought this many times in my life but today, right at this moment, I truly meant it. "Let-me-die. It's enough." I dug my whole hand deeper into the sand, more blood dripped from my nose, more thumping in my ears. I could feel it thumping in the tip of my flesh hand. Let the blood vessels in my brain burst. Let my heart clench so tightly that it cramps and stops. Let it all just *stop*.

They were yelling things and I jumped up, shaking. For a moment, I didn't know if I was coming or going. Seeing out or in. I was rushing back to them before I even knew what I was doing. The four of them stared at me.

"Ask her!" Idris demanded.

DNA was about to speak, but then he noticed my bloody

face, my feet, my eyes. I saw his mouth move, but I just couldn't focus on what he was saying. I felt my eye twitch. "What?" I asked. It was like talking through molasses. Tasiri reached into his pocket and offered me a handkerchief. I took it and wiped my face.

"Are you all right?" DNA asked again.

"Fine," I said, looking at the handkerchief. "Great." The blood I wiped off was at least drying. The bleeding had stopped. I wanted to stick the handkerchief in my ear to wipe the dried blood. "What is it? What are you all shouting about?"

"Ask her," Idris insisted. "Please."

"Look at her," he hissed.

"She's the only one who can help," Idris insisted. The others nodded vigorously. And then they were looking at me.

DNA looked pained as he spoke, "We need you . . . or they want . . . we were thinking . . ."

I heard him, but I didn't hear him. I gazed at him, his face. I was still feeling lightheaded and weird and wrong and broken and adrift, but more importantly looking at his face, albeit pained, actually made me feel better. Rich brown smooth skin, roughened by the wind, clear intense eyes, that angular Fulani nose, DNA was beautiful. Not all things were bad in the world. *I can live in it a little longer,* I thought.

"We need you to connect us to the Bukkaru," Idris loudly said, shoving DNA aside. "Maybe they haven't found all the herdsmen and we can save them. And his sister. Maybe you can connect us through a phone or—"

"Tablet," I said, holding the handkerchief to my nose. It had started to bleed again.

DNA lifted my chin to his face. "If it'll kill you, or even hurt you, I don't—"

"I'll do it," I said. I could do it. I knew that now. Up to this point, I'd used it in small ways. This was different, but I could do it.

DNA's arms tightened on my shoulders. "AO, you don't—"

"But I will," I said. "Look, this happened. That happened. We're happening. For what other reason?"

With his eyes, he pled with me, and I just shook my head and pulled away from him. "Let it be for a reason," I said, stepping around DNA to Idris. "Get me a tablet." I blew my nose hard into the handkerchief, and I felt a gout of blood fill it. I looked apologetically at Tasiri. He held up his hands and said, "You keep." I laughed.

We returned to Force's home because none of us had any devices, except DNA who had a cell phone. But this wasn't a job for a small device. "I need something that can carry power." It also gave me a chance to change out of my bloody clothes, take a nap, eat a large meal. DNA followed me around, looking worried. The shower was a small raised area. It sat above a container that collected the dirty water, strained, recycled, and piped it off to irrigate the fields. You weren't allowed to use anything but raw black soap. I loved this soap, and the shower left me feeling fresh and clean. When I stepped out of the shower, DNA was standing right there holding a towel.

I stood naked before him. Let him see every demarcation, scar, nonhuman part of me. We had already made love and when we did, he'd insisted on touching every part of me, caressing and kissing every part of me that could feel. Let him see me now when he wasn't drunk with need for me. He stood there, holding the towel out as if to catch me. He was staring. After over a minute, I said, "DNA, give me the towel."

Slowly, he stepped forward and wrapped it around me. Then he hugged me close to him. He smelled of palm wine. He'd been drinking. I hadn't known him long, but I knew this was *very* unusual for him. "Please," he said into my ear. "We can find another way. We're in the Hour Glass. There are people here who can hack into *anything*. People love us here. You and I, they'll help if we ask."

"They won't be able to do it quickly," I said. "Every minute matters now. They're killing people."

He hugged me tighter. "You're going to go too far," he said. "You're going to do something. I can see it in your eyes."

I pressed my cheek to his shoulder. *How the hell does he know?* I wondered. He was right. Oh, I planned to do something, all right. I was furious. With my parents. With Ultimate Corp. With DNA's stupid people. With the world. And I had this enormous power that was going to kill me if I truly used it. No, I had this power that was going to kill me. Full stop. Every time I closed my eyes, I connected to them, they were looking back at me, the pomegranate. How could I not DO something with it? And how could my brain and heart endure the power that would flow through me when I did?

"I'm going to convince them to let your sister go and stop killing herdsmen," I said.

"How?"

"I've already found them," I said. "We connect to them, and you all explain. They'll have to listen. You just make sure you speak true."

"Why would they listen to four herdsmen?" he asked.

I said nothing. Instead, I turned my head up, found his lips, and kissed them as I pressed myself to him. "Could you live out here," he asked in my ear, "with me?"

"Just you?" I asked, my lips close to his left ear. I pulled the towel from between us so I could press closer to him. With my left arm, I turned it down and backwards and held the towel behind me, while wrapping my flesh arm around him. My left arm could not lift the towel and, instead, dropped it to the sandy ground.

"Well, maybe with GPS and Carpe Diem and some others," he said. "And an automated vehicle to carry all the mechanical parts you like to tinker with. You could repair people's anti-aejejs, cell phones, tablets."

"Out in the open desert? No roof over my head? Sand storms every few days? A capture station keeping us from dying of thirst?" We'd moved back into the shower, and he was pressing me against the ceramic wall. I turned around and within moments he was inside me, his hand reaching down my waist. I slightly lengthened my legs, so that he could meet me with perfect sweetness. Everything became silver red blue. "Yes," I gasped. "I could." His finger pressed in just the right place, and when I shut my eyes, I didn't care who saw me.

A dream. For the both of us.

═════

We returned to the Mosquito Hut. It was Force's idea. "The computer and software here can handle whatever you're going to do."

I felt foolish. Using my ability to connect to the Bukkaru on an iPad would have been silly. Yes, I could communicate and control the software, but the hardware still had its limits. I didn't blame myself, though. I had a lot on my mind. With the three herdsmen, DNA, me, Force, and Dolapo, it was a tight fit in the small upstairs room. However, with the room-surrounding screens, it didn't feel so bad. According to the wind up clock Dolapo brought, it was seven AM, not long after the sun had come up. The time in the Hour Glass was 10:55.

"I'll do it right after the reset. At 12:11," I said. "I don't want anything to interfere with the connection."

"Where are the cameras?" DNA asked.

"All over," Force said. "There, there, there, there, there, there, there, there, there, there and there." He pointed all around us, at the ceiling, and twice at the floor.

"You all should stand there," I said, pointing to the area that faced the virtual street in front of the building. "There are three cameras in the screen and above. They'll be able to see you as if you were standing right in front of them. I'm turning the other cameras off. Better we control the perspective. I'll only let them see you from the waist up, like on the news."

The four of them wore blue kaftans, tan pants, the traditional conical fiber hats the Fulani were known to wear in the old days. Where Force got them, I didn't know, but judging from how new they looked, they were probably just fashion accessories as opposed to the real thing. Still, they added a nice effect.

DNA was pacing the other side of the room, muttering to himself. They'd all agreed that he'd do the talking. Their message would be clearest if only one of them spoke, and DNA was the "fugitive," the wronged, the brother of the woman they wanted freed. Plus, he had the most to say. Force was speaking to him. Dolapo was laughing and chatting with Idris, Lubega, and Tasiri. I turned to the virtual street and looked up at the virtual sky. The shining sun peeked through occasionally as the blasting and blowing winds of the Red Eye thinned and thickened.

We'd brought washcloths, tissues, ice packs. Force even brought a heart defibrillator. All for me. I didn't think any of it would help, but I kept these thoughts to myself. What I thought about most in that hour were my parents. How they'd looked during that interview. My mother's freshly done braids, her make-up, my father's trimmed beard and the suit I'd never seen him wear. And how relaxed they looked, despite their supposed outrage. My parents loved me, but they'd never liked me. My brother couldn't be found for questioning. He couldn't be there just to put in a good word for me. He loved me too. He'd seen me through all the pain and healing and breaking and re-healing; and my choices. But he'd always been a coward. *Fuck them*, I thought, as I followed everyone up the spiral stairs.

I imagined that with each step I took, more of what was mine fell away from me. My childhood. My apartment in Abuja. My joys. My bank accounts. My created online identity. My birth record. My memories. My pain. By the time I stepped into that room, and was surrounded by the screens, I was exactly me in that moment, and I was so much more because the place was buzzing with connections, power, and cameras.

Force had had four folding chairs and a black leather armchair brought up. None of us had to guess who the reclining chair was for. "It spins, too," Force said, sitting in it, reclining and spinning himself around. "You'll have a 360 degree view of what you see," he said. "You'll be able to zoom in anywhere."

I nodded. The Bukkaru were being smart. They weren't using mobile phones or tablets or anything that gave off a digital signal. Not for now. They'd gone completely analogue. But this was the desert and someone in the desert *always* had a drone. If not in the council camp, somewhere nearby. With a drone, I could see and hear everything in another way. I sat down on the arm chair. "Where did you get this?" I asked.

"It's Hour Glass made," Dolapo said, setting a metal folding chair beside me. She reached into a box beside the chair. "And I brought you snacks, cigarettes, tea, and refreshing mint-scented hemp lotion, all also Hour Glassmade."

"I don't smoke."

"Good," she said, dropping the pack back in the box.

While Force showed them where the cameras were and Dolapo went through her little checklist to make sure she had everything (she seemed to be the one who'd organized all the fine details), I sat down in the chair and reclined. The ceiling was painted black and dotted with white specks that looked like stars. I felt good, calm, though I knew if I blew my nose, clumps of coagulated blood would fly out. And, even if I wanted to blow my nose, I could barely raise my cybernetic arm to do so.

DNA and the others were huddled together talking. I hadn't asked him what he'd say. That part of it wasn't anything I could help with, plus I had other things to worry about. "I hope his speech is good," I muttered.

When it was five minutes to the reset, Force came to me. "You ready?"

I shrugged. "Doesn't matter."

"Find the drone, connect them, and hold," he said. "Let them do the rest. Things get most taxing when you try to do too much at the same time. The human brain isn't a computer, it's *alive*, organic. It's not made to process all that."

"I know," I said. "I don't enjoy nose bleeds, brain damage, or heart attacks, Force."

"Please, AO."

"I know."

"And I know you."

"I'm just going to connect them."

He nodded and stepped to the control center. He sat on the stool, his arms across his chest because there was nothing left for him to do at the moment.

DNA came and knelt beside me. "Do you know what you're going to say?" I asked.

"Yes. I'll be speaking in Pulaar. I'll narrate our innocence, review our tribal code, and . . ." He got up. "Honestly, I don't know if this'll work, but we'll do our best." He bent down and kissed me. "Let this place do the work. Keep it simple. Just connect us."

I watched him go and take his seat. "It's simple, all right," I muttered, watching the clock count down to a second before 1:11. The virtual view of the Hour Glass near sunset became obscured with dust and sand. DNA and the others held hands. Dolapo said, "Here we go." Force sat in his spot looking at me. My left arm twitched, but that was all. I felt good. I felt strong. I was clear. After sixty seconds, I shut my eyes. And then I was sweeping, searching for a drone in the northwestern part of the Nigerian desert.

CHAPTER 18

Bukkaru

It was like flying and taking candy from a baby. I was looking out over miles and miles of sand dune. A glorious bird's eye view. Oh how nice it was to see the sun and open blue sky. I took the moment to enjoy the drone's 3D perspective. It had a fully charged battery and a good camera, one that picked up the sound of the wind but also the distant laughter of the girl below who was looking up at me. She wore a green veil and a loose green dress. She was about ten years old. I could see her dark brown face as she smiled up at me, the drone controls in her hands. Not far behind her was the Bedouin-style black tent, where a woman who was most likely her mother sat reading from a tablet, and a man who was most likely her father was laying out flat black solar panels beside the tent.

I saw the girl's smile drop from her face as I took her drone higher. She looked at her controls and then back up at the drone. Then she began shouting and running after me. Her father was calling his daughter's name, it was Naziha, and telling her to stop. Interesting that he spoke English. She couldn't keep up and soon I had taken little Naziha's drone, to be used for more important things.

Once I was ready, it was easy to gather the Bukkaru. They'd grown comfortable in 24 hours, each person secretly switching on their cell phones and tablets, sure that no one would notice and anxious to see what was going on in the world, to watch streaming series, check in on friends. I sent messages to every single one of them.

"**No point in switching off. We've found you. Gather, so we can talk. Ten minutes. Sincerely, DNA and the Last Herdsmen.**" For good measure, I locked their devices and watched as most of them rushed with their devices to a central location in the Bukkaru council camp. People bring their tech everywhere with them. Why it didn't dawn on them to leave it behind was just a sign of these foolish times.

"I've found and alerted them," I said. "They're gathering. Wait a few minutes."

"How are you feeling?" Dolapo asked.

"Her heart rate is still normal," Force said from where he sat.

"Feel fine," I said. My lips felt heavy, my whole body felt heavy. I was mostly with the drone, which was still flying toward the camp. I put the images from the drone and from all the gathering devices on all the screens for everyone in the room to see. Only the drone image was steady, the images from mobile phone and tablet cameras in constant motion.

"Look at that," Force said.

"Can they see or hear us?" Dolapo asked.

"No," I said.

"The image from above is the drone, so you found one?" DNA asked.

"Easily," I said. I slowly opened my eyes and sat up to look at all the camera connections I'd unlocked. All around me were boxes showing what people were doing, shaky images as people walked, stood with their phones in hand, near black screens from phones in pockets, people seeming to peer at us as they looked at their tablets or phones. Ninety eight screens. The biggest being the drone's bird's eye view.

You could see it happening. All the screen images were doing ninety-eight separate things. Then gradually, every single one of them began to show or move to the same place—the center of the camp. It was uncanny. And once the drone I'd stolen arrived, hovering far above, we could see them all gathering. All the points of view told pieces of the same story. I hadn't expected everyone in the camp to jump up and gather so quickly though.

"Have they been expecting this?" I asked, sitting back on the chair.

"Doesn't matter now," DNA said. "You all ready?"

The herdsmen nodded and straightened up. We watched as more faces began to appear in their screens. An old man with rich brown skin wearing a plain tan kaftan looked into one of the screens. "That's a member of the Bukkaru," DNA said.

I lowered the drone to the point where people began to look up and point. What looked to be about fifty people had gathered. Sixty-five to be exact. Sixty-six. The herdsmen began to point and speak in Pulaar at the same time. "That's the Bukkaru," Idris said. "They have gathered. Start it!"

"Who?" I asked. "Which ones? Point them out."

They were gathered farthest from the camp, the people streaming out to face them. It was obvious who the Elders were. Important-looking men wearing important clothes being looked at by everyone else because they were important.

I glanced at DNA, and he nodded.

"Your heartrate is still normal," Force said. "Remember to breathe."

I felt Dolapo reach forward and squeeze my arm. When I closed my eyes, she put her hand on my shoulder. "Keep it there," I said.

"Okay."

Inhale, exhale.

I hovered before the Bukkaru and they looked right at us. It was as if they were facing DNA and the others. I checked the drone to see if I could channel their voices through it. I could. First I sent a message. It was for the Bukkaru, but I sent it to every single phone, tablet, tv, screen. "We speak. You listen. Here is the truth." I turned on the cameras in front of DNA, Idris, Tasiri and Lubega. Then I put the four of them on every screen in that camp. Everyone, including the Bukkaru members looked down at their screens.

DNA began speaking in Pulaar. I could have had his words instantly translated. He'd launched right into what sounded like a passionate speech. I was certainly interested. However, I just didn't think it would work. Why would common sense work for a people who'd just turned around and started killing the oldest part of themselves? Because of what was clearly a bloody violent misunderstanding. No. I had a better plan. I hadn't shared it with any of them, not even DNA. I executed it now.

Ultimate Corp. It always came down to this fucking corporation. I needed to show these people its involvement in their affairs. Let them all see, too. I went to the pomegranate. While the others were focused on the meeting. While my brain dialogued with those who were connected to my brain. While I made sure the drone stayed steady, the connections remained, the cameras were on. My nose started bleeding.

The pomegranate took my command and then off I went. It was easy once I decided to look for the millions of files. They took me through thousands. I found the connections I needed. But then, well, I wasn't *looking* for this particular bit of pivotal information. It was coincidence. Maybe. The pomegranate helped me interpret it. *Oh this is good.*

Then I found and connected phones owned by Ultimate Corp executives to the Bukkaru meeting. Fifteen of them. Three of those executives were Nigerian. They would know exactly what they were seeing. They'd tell the others. They'd have to pay attention now.

And the "coincidental" document. I had it. And it made something terrible as clear as a calm day in the desert. I was flying faster, like electricity. A part of me, at least. With that document. Everything has a record. In some way. This one was a recording of a meeting. I came back to myself and realized someone was standing on my chest. My eyes flew open, and I was looking right into Force's eyes, he was carrying the defibrillator pads. "Wha . . . ?" I said.

"You're going to have a heart attack!" he whispered. Dolapo was beside him, weeping quietly. DNA and the others were focused on the part of the screen before them. I was still holding the connection. One of the Bukkaru elders was standing now. He seemed to be shouting at them through the drone camera. DNA's sister Wuro stood beside him, looking angry. Her hands were tied together.

I let my body go limp. Closed my eyes. Inhaled, exhaled. Force was still whispering angrily at me. My ears felt wet. My left shoulder was burning. I zipped off, again. If this was my death, let me finish what I was doing first. Ultimate Corp had it coming. At the moment I sent it, the Bukkaru Elder was still shouting. It was the perfect time for the footage to cut in.

The Ultimate Corp symbol was in the top left corner. Along with the date of twenty years ago, days after June 15th, the Day of the Four Herdsmen, the incident in which four so-called Fulani herdsman entered a village and killed and robbed everyone in it and then set it aflame. The Day of The Four Herdsmen put all Fulani herdsmen in Nigeria back on the global radar as terrorists.

"Who's going to stick up for them?" a thin-lipped man in a sharp suit said, sitting back on a plush leather chair that creaked under his ample weight. "These guys are off the grid, *born* off the grid. No citizenship, no identity, thus no digital trail. They're solitary, always covered in dust, Africans are afraid of Africans already. Plus, these herders have been viewed for decades as terrorists. So let's take this new incident and up the ante. We pay off a couple hundred more of them to give up herding cows and instead shoot up towns. *POOF!* Threat to Ultimate Corp's commerce in the north gone, and we can continue building. Hell, imagine all the beef we can sell there."

"Maybe. But those people really aren't a threat, per se. They just . . ."

The thin-lipped man leaned in, his cheeks flushing with excitement. He pointed a finger at the other man who didn't seem remotely intimidated. "You want an environment where there's control and order and not chaos, you get rid of past problems and arguments, all the history nonsense. Replace it with creature comfort, convenience. Trust me, this'll work. Even the wildest people relax when they're content. Everyone wins."

The slimmer man was smiling and nodding now. "These are certainly some wild people."

Chuckles.

They'd planned it. Amplified it. Manipulated it. The last

few true Fulani herdsmen with their old simple ways, fresh milk and meat and nomadic lifestyle, had suffered for it. And Ultimate Corp had been arrogant enough to record and store this conversation where someone could hack into, steal, and broadcast it. Ultimate Corp was powerful and wicked, but it didn't worry enough. The recording froze on the face of a smirking executive. I put his first sentence on repeat, "Who's going to stick up for them?"

I could hear shouts of shock and outrage in the Bukkaru camp. DNA and the others were all standing, staring at me.

"Where'd you find that?" DNA was shouting.

"Just found it," I said. I was fading. "Accident. Coincidence. Karma." I coughed and my lips were wet with what? Blood? Who knew. Who cared. I was done. The drone was still hovering. Everyone was shouting outrage. Everyone was listening. Good. A glass of cosmic milk from the great cosmic cow.

For me, all went black.

———

I awoke to the spicy smell of pepper soup. I had a strong feeling of deja-vu and, my eyes still closed, I tried to grasp at it. But it slid, slithered, and then slipped away. I found myself looking into the millions of eyes of the pomegranate. I opened my eyes. I was sitting on my recliner, the screens around me showing the Hour Glass again. From the darkening of the sky I could glimpse through the storm's dust, the sun was setting. DNA was sitting on a low chair slouched beside me eating from a bowl of what had to be pepper soup. He didn't seem surprised to see me awake.

"Are you hungry?" he asked. He picked up a piece of goat

meat from his bowl and bit into it. "No idea who made this but Dolapo gave it to me and it's delicious."

When I spoke, my mouth felt as if it had been shot with Novocain and I slurred my words. "Wha'happened?"

"You mean after you basically called for war?" But he was grinning. He bit into more of his meat. He was ravenous and enjoying the fact that he had an appetite.

"Eh? Where's everyone?"

"Here and there. It's been a few hours," he said with a shrug. "How do you feel?"

I sat up and that was when I noticed it. "Oh!" I shook my arm and it flopped limply at my side. My left arm. My cybernetic arm was dead. I shook it again. "Shit," I said.

He bit into his goat meat and said nothing as he watched me.

I scrambled to my feet. I shook and shook my arm. Nothing. I was as I'd been when I was little, a girl with only one working arm. I wanted to scream. Instead, I looked at my flesh hand. I made a fist. I felt a little better.

DNA spoke calmly as he put his bowl of soup down beside his chair and stood up. "Your nose was bleeding," he said. "Your ears were bleeding, then you passed out. Your arm . ." He looked at it. "There was so much happening. The connection was still there, and we were all seeing each other, hearing each other, feeling each other's outrage. The Bukkaru were all yelling, people were on their feet, Force was cursing, the other herdsmen were shouting with the Bukkaru, Dolapo was crying, but I was watching *you*. Your robot arm started jerking around. Sparks, heat, then it just stopped. How does it feel now?"

"Like nothing."

"Doesn't hurt?"

"No." I shut my eyes and I was gazing at the pomegranate which was always gazing at me. Pain was the doorway, the permission, the allowance. I'd have taken pain over nothing any day. I needed to focus on something else. Within seconds I knew what it would be. I opened my eyes. "I've started a war."

"Yes," DNA said, the smile returning to his face.

"Your sister Wuro?"

"Safe with my parents."

I smiled. "And I saved the remaining herdsmen."

"Yes."

"Will Idris, Tasiri, and Lubega stay in the Hour Glass?"

"No. They'll leave the Hour Glass and join the few remaining herdsmen gathering in Niger."

"So they weren't all killed."

"Many were. Most were. But no, not all. I won't be joining them."

"I exposed Ultimate Corp."

"Yes," he said, with a small smile. "People reposted that footage. With important *context*. It's already gone viral worldwide."

I nodded, shaking my arm again. Still nothing. "People will still buy from and do business with Ultimate Corp. They'll still schedule their damn warehouse tours and post video and photos from there, keeping the myth alive."

"Oh, of course," he said. "It's never that easy. The execs in that footage were right. People don't care, as long as they are comfortable and life is made easy. Most." He took me in his arms. We were still like this when Force came up the stairs. When he saw me, his face brightened. "Oh good! You're awake! You okay?"

"My arm has shut down," I said, shaking the thing like a dead snake. Now that the arm was shut off, it felt so heavy. I'd

have to work hard not to stumble to the left when I walked or
ran. I certainly wouldn't be able to sleep on my other side.

"What's broken can be fixed," he said. "There are doctors
here who can repair it. Even upgrade it. Better doctors than
you'll probably find on the outside."

"There's no time," I said.

"There will be. When all this is over."

I smiled. *If I'm alive*, I thought.

"For now," DNA said, pulling a piece of red blue Ankara
cloth from his pocket like a magician. "Tie it up with this, so
the flesh isn't pulled by the weight. Dolapo gave it to me." He
wrapped it over my shoulder and when he stood back, my arm
was secured in a sling. The excessive weight of it was a *lot* more
manageable now.

"I guess this'll do," I said. The three of us stood there for a
moment, me with my sling. DNA had picked up his bowl of
pepper soup and spoon, and Force was frowning. Then at the
same time, we looked away from each other.

"I'll check your vitals," Force said, picking up his tablet.
DNA sat in my recliner, finishing his pepper soup while Force
stuck sensory pads on me.

"I feel okay," I said, looking at the sensory pads on my chest.
He put one on my forehead and then on the back of my neck.
I'd braided my dreadlocks into two braids to expose my neural
implant's silver nodule. He stuck a sensor on that, too.

"The problem with you," Force said, "is that you're so used
to pain and discomfort that your definition of feeling okay is
not the greatest indicator of being okay."

"Exactly," DNA said, putting his empty bowl on the floor.

"I know my body better than either of you," I snapped.
"I'm the one who lives in it. And I say I feel good. Really good.
Except for this." I pointed at my useless arm in a sling.

"Shh, don't move," Force said. "It's reading."

My brain scan would show extensive damage. Maybe whole networks of nerves in the left side of my body would be dead. It would tell me that my heartbeat was irregular. My blood pressure would be elevated into the red zone. I was on the verge of five strokes. It would show short-circuiting in my legs, thanks to the power surge from my arm.

"Jesus!" Force whispered.

My eyes grew wide. I didn't want to hear. DNA was on his feet. "What do we do?" he said.

"No, no, no," he said. "Relax. Breathe, AO. You have to stay even."

"Then don't—"

"Force, what is it?" DNA insisted. He was standing over him, looking at his tablet.

"She's okay," Force said. "Her blood pressure is a little high, but aside from that, no problems with brain activity, no ruptures, everything is fine!" So somehow my heart had gone from cardiac arrest to being stabilized after I'd passed out. No damage. No nothing. Was my body adjusting to the changes in my brain?

I didn't think before I did it. There was only one way to find out, and if I thought about it, I'd be too afraid to try. I went in to face the pomegranate of eyes.

There they were, all looking right at me, me looking at them. They heard and then showed me. When I opened my eyes, I looked at DNA, a small drop of blood falling from my nostril, and said, "The term, Fulani herdsmen, is the most searched term on the Internet right now. Second is my name. Journalists have shown up at the burned Ultimate Corp warehouse, and there are photos of the drones and soldiers I shut down. There was a dust storm not long after we left, so everything was covered with sand. The downed drones looked like forgotten artifacts, and the robot soldiers looked like dead men who'd died peacefully. And . . ." I paused to take a breath. I chuckled. Oh the irony. "And Ultimate Corp stocks are at a record high."

CHAPTER 19

The Market

I wasn't the one who wanted to go to the market. DNA did. But I was all for it. We'd been in the Hour Glass for three days, and I was sinking. It wasn't just what I'd *been* through, it was my conversation with Force about the role Ultimate Corp had played in me being the way I was. And it was what I was *going* through. I couldn't sleep, not alone. Every time I closed my eyes, all the eyes of the AIs were there. In my sleep, I'd speak to them, and they'd think back. They'd show and take me places. Thousands of places, within moments. It wasn't the going, it was the *number* of goings.

And each time I returned, DNA would be beside me, gazing at me, sitting up. Frowning. My face would be wet with tears and sweat, and he'd tell me I'd been weeping and saying over and over, "Slow, slow, slow down, slow down, slow down." And when I was awake, when the headaches came, I wished I was asleep. Thumpa thumpa, thumpa no matter what I was doing, when they descended on me, I was to stop, sit, inhale, exhale, relax. Force's girlfriend, Dolapo taught me how to do it. Not only was she a coder, but in her "previous life" she'd been an EMT, a high stress job that caused her to look into meditation.

"You can control your heart rate with it," she said on the second day. Maybe DNA had said something to her, or maybe someone else had heard me sleeping. The place they lived in was practically communal, everyone sleeping in areas close to one another. There was no rain in the Hour Glass, so everyone slept out in the open beneath the restrained storm above.

We sat in a space amongst some cannabis bushes she was growing. The people in the Hour Glass smoked, ate, wove cloth with a lot of this and Dolapo had three lush and well-lit gardens growing three different strains. The plants we sat amongst were flowering and smelled like a parade of bothered skunks.

"Close your eyes," she said.

"I don't like to do that," I said. "I know that sounds weird."

She shook her head. "I understand. Force told me some of it. Sorry, I forgot." She looked to her side. "See these plants? They're beautiful, aren't they? Focus on them. Their veins, the points on their leaves."

I nodded and stared at the green hand shaped leaves.

"Take a deep breath," she said. And then after a few seconds, "Now let it out slowly. Think only about those leaves. The number of leaves, breathe in their earthy smell. Be here. Be now."

The eyes were still there, but there were thirty second intervals where all I actually thought about were the leaves. All I smelled was their scent. All I heard was their rustle. It was glorious, and the first time I was able to achieve this, I cried.

The day we went to the market was an hour after one of my sessions with Dolapo, and I was feeling clear. Dolapo had lent me more of her clothes and I was wearing jeans, a black t-shirt, and a white veil. She'd even given me a pair of her giant Jupiter shaped earrings after I saw them and commented that they were beautiful.

When DNA asked me if I wanted to go, I wasn't connecting things. It was only as we walked into the people and motion that I started frowning. People were looking at me, talking and pointing. But people were also greeting Force and patting me on the shoulder. I'd never been to this place and everyone seemed so friendly and welcoming. A woman selling herbs and spices gave me a necklace of fragrant smelling herbs. She'd put it over my head, her face coming so close to mine. "Welcome, AO." She smelled of curry and the herbs she gave me smelled of mint and sage.

"Where can I get a connection?" DNA was asking Force as we moved through the crowded market. "I need to reach my family."

"I don't see why I can't just—"

"No, AO," DNA said.

"Agreed. Plus, finding a phone is easy and cheap here," Force said. "Follow me. I know a guy."

DNA held my hand, and I wrapped my white veil more tightly around me as we moved through the people. We passed a group of young men sitting on a car that was, for some reason, parked right in the middle of the busy market. The young men were dressed like Fulani or Hausa, but they smiled at me and called to me in Igbo, "Agu nwanyi! Agu nwanyi!" They all fell to their knees, still chanting. This actually made me laugh and my laughter was rewarded with blown kisses. This annoyed DNA, and I laughed some more.

"You didn't believe me. They love you here," Force said. "I told you."

I stood behind DNA and Force as the programmer scheduled a connection for DNA with his parents. DNA was holding the tablet as the connection was made. He wasn't focused on me. Force wasn't focused on me. Most in the area had gotten their fill of me. The hand fell on my shoulder and in that moment, I realized I couldn't see through any of the cameras around me. Not a cell phone, personal security camera or tablet. Nothing. I was being blinded. I was surrounded.

"What?" I turned to see who was grasping my shoulder. The grasp squeezed hard and I knew I was in trouble. I stumbled back, bumping into DNA. Someone ripped off my necklace of herbs. Then there was a wild struggle and press of bodies. Hands snatched and grabbed at me and then were pulled away. I punched and kicked and nearly went down. I couldn't tell what the hell was happening. Then I stumbled and my body slammed against something. I heard DNA shouting for me and he sounded way too far away. Hands and bodies pressed me against the car. I caught the eye of one of the young men who'd been here when we arrived. He was wrestling with someone wearing a grinning masquerade face, except instead of wood, it was made of gold foil.

"Get on top of the car!" the young man yelled. "Get—" The masked person came at me and the young man was wrestling him again. Similar fights were breaking out all around me. I was being attacked, but people were fighting for me, too! What was it with me and markets? I twisted and grabbed at the car with my good arm. I stumbled onto the hood of the car, then onto its roof. I caught my balance and stood up straight, my white veil fluttering in the wind. When had it gotten windy? My metal feet made dents in the car's roof but that was the least of my worries. I could see all the chaos clearly from here.

DNA was feet away, trying to shove in my direction. Men with golden masks surrounded me, except they couldn't get past my protective perimeter of market people. And these men and women were pushing back. The wrestling was getting more intense as the gold-faced men realized they couldn't get to me. Then I was able to see everything from above. I looked up.

A drone, one I could control. I brought it down with a mere thought, turning off its camera eye. It was an Ultimate Corp drone. This was Ultimate Corp? What the fuck were they trying to do?! And how had they been able to blind me? To stop me from seeing through all the cameras?

A ripple of hot and electric rage shot through my body. All the eyes swiveled and for a moment, I felt as if I were in so many places at the same time that my rage felt a thousandfold. A millionfold. I pulled myself in. These golden faced idiots could hurt DNA. That was enough to focus my mind. I stamped my foot on the top of the car so hard that it made a deep dent. This got almost everyone's attention. I did it again.

"HEY!!" I shouted. "Look at ME!!" I removed my white veil and pulled off the band holding my locks together. I shook out my locks so everyone could see the silver nodule in the center of my head. "See me! AO! The woman with the nerve to kill the men trying to kill her!"

The fighting continued for another minute, gold-faced people pushed and shoved at the people protecting me on all sides. One of them punched a woman in the face and as she crumbled to the ground, a man leapt at the gold-faced man who'd punched her.

I was breathing heavily now, and I could hear my heart pounding in my head, ears, chest, doing a beat that I'd never heard. Tripped up, staccato, wrong. My vision blurred, the world swimming around me—no, not swimming, blowing. The fighting at my feet was growing wilder, the car beginning to shake. I was going to faint and fall off the car. I had to breathe. Ah, there it was. Ultimate Corp couldn't help themselves. They'd thought they had me, and they had planned to record it. That's why that drone had been there. And maybe they'd planned to show the world the capture of the crazy insane wild woman. Arrogant. They were always so arrogant.

A pain shot down my arm. Still, I found and flew their drone directly over me in moments, then had it move down and hover a few feet in front of me. And in this moment, everything died down, the gold-faced people looking away from the drone. Those directly in its line of vision, scrambled for cover like cockroaches. I wished the drone's camera had been panoramic. *See me*, I thought. *Make them all see me*. There was no time to push for all of Nigeria to witness all this through this camera, let alone the entire globe. However, I connected it to over half of Nigeria, all of Lagos.

"Cannabis plants," I whispered. "Please." I inhaled deeply. And they showed me. Fields and fields of it, waving at me in the breeze, seeking my attention. Just for a moment. Over there. Back at Force and Dolapo's home. I inhaled deeply. And let the breath out slowly. Again. I inhaled, then I looked directly into the camera eye. "Do I make you feeeeeel uncomfortable? Unsafe?" I snarled. "Have you called all your loved ones to check on them? You want to know why you feel that way? You want to know who's to blame for *me*?? The same people who made your mobile phones. The same people who made your children's toys. The company who sells you the supermeats you put in your husband's okra soup and pounded yam."

Breathe, I thought.

"*They* are responsible for me. How did we get to this?" I paused. "Olives. If you do not remember the Ultimate Corp olives that caused five children to be born with horrible deformities, rush to the internet, look it up. The stories are all there. I am one of those children. You see, my mother loved olives. Especially when she was pregnant. Maybe it was the salt, or the taste, the nutty flavor olives are famous for. Or the firm fruit texture.

"And so I was born. With one arm and one arm stump. Legs with unformed femurs and no joints. One lung. My intestines in a knot. They made sure I lived, though. Then when I was fourteen, another so-called 'accident' that crippled me further. I have a cybernetic arm, cybernetic legs, human-made intestines and a human-made lung. I've got neural implants, see my head? I thought I was me because I was me. That I chose all this for myself. But what is choice when you have little choice? It's not just me. It's *you*, too."

Breathe, I thought.

"We have pollen tsunamis because of Ultimate Corp's periwinkle grass campaign in New Calabar. Naija people, which of you owns the land you live on? How many of you are Ultimate Corp academic scholars? Vomiting up rhetoric for your PhDs. Those few of you privileged enough to make it to university, are you studying what you want to study or are you studying so you can do what makes *them* more money? Which of you can *afford* to drop out of university? What are your real dreams? I'm a self-taught mechanic, my parents were professors. Olives."

Breathe, I thought. I turned to look at everyone around me. All eyes on me, outside and inside. They were listening. So many. And I'd ensorcelled them. There was DNA. I turned the camera to him. The gold-faced people moved away from the camera's eye and, in turn, away from DNA. I looked at him as I spoke, but I spoke to the market people of the Hour Glass around me. "People of the Hour Glass. I just got here. I was tired and you embraced me. Thank you." I was calm now. "I've seen what they do."

Someone in the group shouted back. "We all have, girl!"
Even more people shouted more affirmation.

"We've seen what they do," I said again.

"We all have!" More people shouted this.

"We've seen what they do," I said again.

"We all have!" Even more joined.

I grinned, tears welling in my eyes. Days ago they'd tried to
kill me in a market, now here were free wild people protecting
me. "We've seen what they do!" I shouted.

"WE ALL HAVE!" Now there were fists in the air and the
voices sounded hoarse and low, there were mostly men in the
crowd. Now almost everyone was in the market space. I could
see more people coming. Their phones up, recording. Recording me.

In the height of the moment, one of the gold-faced people
leapt on the car. He tried to grab me and out of nowhere, I saw
Dolapo scream, leap and throw herself on the man.

"Dolapo," I shouted. "What are you doing?"

They went down, the man punching at her. I could hear her
grunting in pain, and I was about to throw myself into the mix
when another man grabbed at me. He was very strong. Instead
of twisting away, I grabbed him back with my dead arm
which clearly *wasn't* dead. There was a mad scramble toward
the car, but I was barely aware of it. I was barely aware of anything. My body was acting. Again. Reacting. *Oh no!* My arm
was acting on its own. Again. In my mind, I'd given this phenomenon a name, though it had only happened once. Kill
Mode. I shoved at him with my flesh hand as he tried to grab
me again. Idiot! He managed to get his hands around my
throat. He was choking me but only for a moment, because my
cybernetic arm pulled back and I was pulled back *with* it! Then

I saw my left fist punch the man so hard that it smashed his gold mask.

The market space burst into violence. Shouts and grunts, as people fought and I was pulled back. I fell hard on the ground, my metal hand still in a fist, pressing to my face. It smelled of blood, was wet with it. My left arm buzzed and then went numb again. "Oh," I whispered. Someone was hoisting me up, and suddenly DNA was in my face. He pulled me along, and somehow Force was in front of him pulling *him*, as was a bloody-nosed Dolapo. We were battered left and right, but by the backs of people. The market people were shielding us, giving us a way out as they fought. We arrived at a red car.

"Get in, get in!!" Force shouted.

I threw myself into the backseat with Dolapo and Force and DNA climbed into the front. "Go!" Force said to the car and it went. I was lying on my side, my face to the car seat. I slapped my arm. I might as well have slapped a slab of scrap metal, dead again.

"Dolapo," I breathed. "Are you all right?"

"Better than the other guy," she said, her voice nasally. She sniffed and coughed a laugh. Then she groaned with pain. "I have never fought a man in my entire life."

DNA's sling of cloth hung around my neck, and I tried unsuccessfully to push my arm into it. I peeked outside. "I don't see them following us."

"They will. My God, how the fuck did Ultimate Corp get into the Hour Glass?!" Force asked.

"You all have too much confidence in your privacy," DNA muttered. "When they see a threat to their finances, they'll fly into a pit of fire. They'll just make sure they use fire-proof drones."

"Why are they coming after me so hard?" I asked. "The *government* isn't even here!"

"AO," Force said. "You can control tech with your mind."

"Badass," Dolapo said, pinching her nose and tilting her head back.

The drones were about a fourth of a mile away and gaining fast.

"They'll taser the entire car, knock us all out. Shit," Force said. He looked hard at me. "Get rid of them, AO."

"Already have. They're gone," I said. I rolled over and grabbed my arm and shook it. Nothing.

"Good," he said. "We have a chance then. I have a plan."

DNA, Dolapo, and I leaned in.

———

Force's plan for us was insane.

"Stop looking at me like that," he said. "I mean, think about it, it's all you really can *do*. If you don't go . . ." He didn't need to finish what he was saying. The Hour Glass had been infiltrated by Ultimate Corp operatives. I could see them now that I knew to look. They were everywhere. Except where we were driving. Nothing was where we were driving. Not a camera, not a drone, not even a person with a mobile phone. Within a mile radius. We were driving down a paved road so black that it could have been laid down yesterday. The land around us was populated by thousands of heliostatic mirrors, each the size of a car.

"This was a Sunflower Initiative Solar Farm before the Red Eye started," Dolapo said. "The power tower was at the center of these mirrors but it was blown down long ago."

"It's a total dead zone now," I said.

"Has been for a while," Dolapo said. "The Oracle Solar Complex wanted to harvest the parts but—"

I gasped. "We're at the edge, aren't we?" I said. I could see it. Literally see it. The digital shield of the anti-aejej. To my new senses, it looked like billions of tiny pink jelly-like things wriggling about to form the shield. It was making a soft hissing sound. And beyond were the swirling violent winds. Force stopped the car right where the road continued into the storm.

The four of us sat there, silent. The four of us knew. "Okay," DNA finally said. He got out of the car. I turned to Force. "They get you, you're done," he said.

"I know."

"You have something that scares the shit out of them," Force said. "You threaten their existence. You just exposed them to—"

"All of West Africa," I said. "On mobiles, TVs, tablets, oh, why'd I do that? Why'd I—"

"Do NOT second guess yourself," Dolapo said.

"Agreed," Force said. "Own your actions. Always."

DNA slapped a hand at the window. "We need to do this," he shouted. "Come on, AO."

I jumped as sirens started to sound.

"Force," Dolapo said, looking at him with wide eyes. Force didn't seem surprised at all.

"AO, go!" he said.

I looked and I saw it flash in my mind, a symbol in the shape of infinity. Dolapo was shouting in Yoruba. She'd let go of her nose and blood was dripping out and still she shouted at Force to hurry.

"Code Red," I said. "Force, what's Code Red?" The symbol was bouncing all over the Hour Glass's local network as a text message.

Ignoring both me and Dolapo, Force leaned out of the truck. "DNA, you have my anti-aejej?"

"What?" I said. "Anti-aejej? What's going on?!"

"I do," DNA said, grabbing it from a back pack I'd never seen before. "Wish we had masks, too!" All I had was the water bottle I'd been carrying in my pocket before this all happened. Deep pockets will always be the best thing about clothes.

"I didn't think it would be like this! Turn it on! Turn it on!" Force said, clicking his seatbelt. "Go! The Hour Glass anti-aejej is about to shut down!"

"Are you crazy?!" Dolapo shouted.

Force looked at her with eyes so full of rage that Dolapo immediately shut up.

"What?!" DNA shouted, rushing back to the truck.

"Force," I said, grasping the car window. "Wait, wait, why?!"

"Because I sent the command! In five minutes. It'll stay down for exactly four minutes. That's enough time to send a bunch of those damn soldiers to a flying death or trap them where they can't come after you. You'll have a head start. But you need to get moving!"

"Will you be all right?"

"No!" Dolapo shouted. "We'll be—"

"This car's weighted to withstand the winds," he said, but the look on his face didn't convince her. "We'll be okay. We always are. Everyone knows to go underground if they hear sirens. And the shelters are all over, it's hard to be far from one. Some of the soldiers will try to follow people in; there are going to be fights."

We moved back as he wildly turned the car around. He stopped and waved to us. "Make all this count, AO. Go!" he said. "Before you *can't*." Then he and Dolapo were off, sending up a huge wake of dust.

I turned to DNA. "I don't . . . people are going to die! I can't have that on my conscience. The Hour Glass is run by an AI; Maybe I can—"

"Don't, AO!" DNA said, his eyes wild. He grabbed the front of my shirt and pulled me to his face. "Are you *trying* to kill yourself? I've been wondering this for a while now!"

"I'm not," I said, staring at him. My dead arm nearly slipped out of the sling. "I just—"

"Did you already forget yesterday!"

The dust from Force's car still floated around us. The sirens blared. It had been a week since the morning I'd left my apartment to go and buy ingredients for a quiet dinner.

I grabbed my hair and sighed loudly. "I'm . . . I'm sorry.".

"Why?"

"I don't know."

I tied my locks back, covering the silver nodule in the middle of my head as he held up the anti-aejej and turned it on. I could feel it immediately, and it was much stronger than the one DNA owned and had left behind at Force and Dolapo's place. I shivered, feeling a staticky itch in the back of my throat that tasted like the smell of those sheets of fabric softener my mother liked to use.

"What happens now?" I asked. "What if someone is outside without protection?"

"Like Force said, it's happened before," he said. "That's why there are sirens. People know how to not just survive, but *live* here."

We were facing away from the border, so we saw it happen. It was like a great beast pausing for a moment to admire the meal it was about to enjoy and then swallowing it in one gulp. When the anti-aejej was on, because it was early afternoon of the day, you could see sunlight peeking through the top of the dome, the storm blustering over its surface. We were far enough from all the Hour Glass villages with their buildings and out-door communal dwellings, so the moment the anti-aejej went off we were able to watch the dust and wind attack. It was like watching the end of the world.

We rushed to the border. We were going to die out there.

CHAPTER 20

Anti-Aejej

We didn't feel the blast of the wind, but it was like moving from life into death in a tiny bubble. We huddled together as we moved, shuffling farther and farther from the safe danger of the Hour Glass. Behind us was the Hour Glass, a place that had been a safe space, with atmosphere and sanity before we'd arrived. Now it was momentarily a chaos of brown red violent undulating shadow. But there were no shelters where we were going. The reality of it all overwhelmed me, and I fell to my knees, breathing heavily. DNA grabbed my arm.

"Get up," he shouted. "Get up!! They'll realize soon. We have to get as far as we can!"

"They won't come," I gasped. "Easy to let us die out here."

It wasn't completely still in our anti-aejej's protection. There was a soft breeze and the air smelled almost sooty, as if it were waiting for even the slightest reason to burst into flame. I coughed, digging my hand into the soft sand. Why was the sand warm? I let him help me up. He grasped my dead arm and when he let go, I felt so weighed down. The dead arm was so so heavy. "Okay," I said. We started moving again.

It was like being on another planet. Maybe Mars during one of its planet consuming storms, or better yet, Jupiter. Witnessing the fury and chaos up so close that you could touch it. If I reached through the barrier of the anti-aejej with my flesh and bone hand, would I pull it back in as only bone? *At least it would match my other arm*, I thought.

We walked and walked. At some point, DNA started singing a song in Pulaar, his voice travelling no farther than to the edge of the force field two feet in front of us. It bounced back and travelled two feet behind us and bounced back to our left and right. Nowhere to go.

But his voice was sweet and I shut my eyes as we walked, and I listened. And behind my eyes, I could see that we were truly stranded for miles and miles and miles, unless we turned back. We could not turn back. And then we heard the beeping.

"What is that?" DNA asked. I could barely hear him, but I didn't really have to. We'd been quiet for two hours. I don't know what was going through his head. He'd stopped singing. Neither of us had taken even a gulp of the one bottle of water we had. We weren't thirsty.

I couldn't answer at first. I needed to stay with it for a moment. I took a deep breath, feeling my blood pressure wanting to rise. I reached out to them and was quickly told, there was no way to wirelessly charge the anti-aejej because it was too old, it hadn't been upgraded with the compatibility. There was no way to squeeze out more energy from its dying battery, either, because it had gone beyond its emergency stores an hour ago. I stopped walking.

"We're doomed."

"Goddammit, there's no sunlight here, otherwise, it would charge," DNA said. "It was supposed to last a LOT longer than this!"

"Force didn't account for the fact that they lose energy when you don't recharge them often. When's the last time he left the Hour Glass? These old ones are such shit." I sighed again. I was so tired and hungry and all my muscles ached.

The anti-aejej beeped again.

"I want to say he should have known better," he sighed and shook his head, looking at the anti-aejej in his hands. The screen was blank except for the green flashing dot that indicated it was working but not for long. "All too fast. All too fast."

I coughed and rubbed my face. "Think, think, think," I muttered. But there was nothing. We had nothing. Nothing but my bottle of water. Nothing but ourselves. We were going to die. As if to confirm this, the anti-aejej beeped again, and this time a number appeared on its small screen. Fifteen. We had fifteen minutes. We grasped each other's hands and looked deep into each other's eyes.

"You were great back there," he said. "I don't think the company will ever be viewed the same way."

I smiled. "We've exposed them."

He nodded. "Long overdue. For the herdsman, nomad culture, the people of the Hour Glass, and all those the company has crippled, including you." He reached out and took my good hand and drew me close. As we embraced and I lay my head on his shoulder and he lay his on mine. Two minutes later, the forcefield grew smaller with us.

"They own everything," I said.

"So they thought."

I laughed. "Until I started glitching." And I swear in that moment, if all of them could laugh, they did. I pressed my body to him, and smelled his sweaty dusty skin, and it was then that I had an idea. It wouldn't save our lives. We were going to die. But that was okay if this idea worked. It would be more than worth it. I reached out and there I was before the pomegranate of eyes. Millions of them. Attentive. They started looking the moment I had the thought. And then I had my answei. I stood back from DNA and took his hand with my flesh and bone hand. "Come on. We have to move fast."

"Where?" But he let me lead him.

"We're close and we have just enough time if we move now."

We put our heads down and we shuffled. Paying close attention to the border of the anti-aejej. As its strength weakened, it shrunk and our feet got closer and closer to stepping over the edge. We could see nothing with our eyes, but they showed me by other means and I could see it clearly. We were so close. One of the turbines. A Noor.

===

When I was a small child, I thought a lot about dying. What it would feel like. The last thing I would say. The last thing I would think. Where I would be when it happened. I knew I didn't want to be in a hospital room or in the bedroom where I'd spent so much of my miserable life in pain. I wanted to be in the light, basking in the cleansing spirit of the sun. To be in sunlight was to dance. I couldn't dance now, and the sun above was blocked by a chaos of roiling dust and sand and wind. I'd never see the sun again.

I wanted to sit down and wallow in this fact before the anti-aejej quit. Instead, I focused everything I had left on putting one foot in front of the next while holding DNA's hand so tightly it had probably gone numb. "Hurry," I said. We were shuffling now, the dome of the anti-aejej so close that this was all we could do. The tips of DNA's feet were bloody from stepping the tiniest bit into the storm. Not for the first time I was glad to be made of metal in parts that counted.

DNA never asked where we were going. I didn't have the

breath to explain. Let him understand if there was time and reason to understand. The anti-aejej was beeping three minutes when we reached the base of the Noor. The end of the great horizontal helix, where it blasted out accelerated wind and harnessed the power, was not far to the left. But we were at a safe distance. If we'd walked a tenth of a mile to the left, we'd have walked right into the near silent stream and been gloriously obliterated.

We sat with our backs to it. I turned around and touched its surface. Sand-colored and smooth, and cool. I knocked at it with my knuckles. "So solid," I breathed. Even in the noise, I could feel more than hear it, a deep hum.

"Had to be or it would blow away," DNA said, leaning his head back. His face was wet with sweat. The closeness of the dome left the air dusty and hot.

"Why do you think you weren't shot?" I asked. The question had suddenly popped into my mind. When DNA's cattle and friends had been killed in that farmer town, he'd stood there out in the open, in shock, yet no bullet reached him.

"I have wondered, AO," he said. "It was all happening around me, and I willed it and, maybe, something gave my will power."

"Maybe," I said. If there was something I had learned, it was that sometimes, will could be very very powerful. "Two minutes," I whispered. We were still holding hands and I squeezed his tighter.

"AO," he said, looking hard at me. "Do what you came here to do. I won't die until I've seen it done."

I stared at him and he stared back. We'd had so little time together and that time had been spent running for our lives, yet, somehow he knew me so well. He knew what I was. A man my family would see as a mere herdsman who knew so little beyond his patch of desert. One minute and ten seconds.

"Do it," DNA repeated. He laughed and then coughed. The dome had just shrunken some more and the air was foggy with dust. The anti- aejej began to beep the last sixty seconds away. I could already feel the grains of sand getting through as they pelted my face.

"It will hurt, reaching out to so much," I said.

"It's about to hurt a lot more," he said.

I looked up into the chaos above, knowing the Noor was there, near silent and sleek. I turned to DNA. He took me in his arms, and I rested my head on his chest. "It will hurt."

"I know."

"I'm glad I met you."

"I love you," he said, pressing his lips to my ear. I thought about what the sorcerer Baba Sola had said, "The world isn't all about you, AO." Had he known it would come to this? Probably. Maybe that's why he'd wanted to see us with his own eyes. As DNA held me, I reached out. I stepped out, remembering my dream from only days ago. The one with the eyes, so many red eyes. The pomegranate of eyes. I looked back and reached to them and I told them. I did not request. I did not inform. I just acted. I shut them down. Not one by one, all at the same time. I could do that. It was like pressing one button, pulling one plug, sending two commands.

SHUT DOWN. DISCONNECT.

I squeezed my eyes shut as pain like I'd never felt washed over me, flooding my head first. In that spot where they'd placed the chip, where I wasn't supposed to feel pain because there were no nerves. Like fire, like ice, like being torn apart. Into DNA's chest, I screamed and screamed and he held me tighter. I asked for death. I asked for it, then I reached out even further.

Every
　　Single
　　　Fucking
　　　　Noor.

SHUT DOWN. DISCONNECT. SHUT DOWN. DISCON-NECT. SHUT DOWN. DISCONNECT. SHUT DOWN. DIS-CONNECT. "KEEP GOING!" I shouted. "ALL OF YOU, OFF OFF OFF!" I tasted blood in my mouth, felt it fill my ears. My brother's drum beat was wild and beautiful. I would be free of all of it soon. Let my bones, metal and carbon, fly. I coughed, as my heart beat strong and steady in my chest despite the blood dribbling down my nose, from my ears, flooding my mouth. I was crying tears of blood. For myself, for what I should have been, for DNA, his cattle, everyone Ultimate Corp had stunted, deformed, exterminated, and displaced. "Today, you *know* us."

The Noor we leaned against stopped. The hum was there, then it was not. DNA and I looked at each other as the anti-aejej died, then we hugged tightly, pressing our faces into each other's chests as the sand whipped into us. Both of us had just wanted to be left alone to be what we were. Now they had all left us alone to die.

Shhhhhhhhhhhh . . .

I was straining so hard, awaiting the suffocation and sting of the sand on my face that it was several moments before I noticed the sound and the rain. Yes, it was raining. Oh my God, it was raining! Raining . . . sand. We raised our heads, looking at each other as sand fell all around us. Fell, not blew.

The wind had stopped. Noor running all over northern Nigeria
had stopped and now so had the winds of the Red Eye.

I grabbed DNA's hand and pulled, "Run! Or we'll be buried." As we ran, I could see so much.

———

I could see it, though I could only really analyze it later. In the
Hour Glass, everyone who could came out to watch the sand
fall, and those who did not would regret it for the rest of their
lives. Some were still bloody from the market riot that had
been interrupted by the four-minute aejej shut down, but this
did not stop them from bearing witness. The people of the
Hour Glass had resigned themselves to so much in order to be
who they were. They gave up natural sunlight. They gave up a
connection to the rest of the world. They gave up time and endured TIME RESET. They gave up their family and friends.
They gave up space. They'd been used to the swirling chaos that
beat at the anti-aejej dome high above. They were used to the
darkness, the distant noise.

But the rain of sand hitting the dome was a different noise
all together. A steady sound, one that only had one direction,
downward. It collected at the base and people ran to go see.

But before they reached the edges of the Hour Glass, they
stopped to look up instead. There was a woman who threw her
hands up and cried, "Praise Allah!!"

———

I saw because I looked and I had eyes everywhere now. So I saw
the Red Eye close from above, and I zoomed the satellite image
into the storm, and that's how I saw what no other human

being could see. As the sands fell, so did the bones. Finally, those people whose lives had been taken by the Red Eye in the most brutal way—stripped of life, then all flesh—and left to fly and fly, they fell to the ground. All those people could rest. And as the sand fell, all those people were also buried. Finally. Except for a few who tumbled onto and remained on the surface, rib cages, femurs, tibias, humeri, pelvises, skulls, all dust-bleached and wind-blasted a stark white. Scattered all over the Nigerian Sahel Desert. Those bones saw the sun for the first time in a long long time.

———

DNA and I ran, unable to see anything before us or around us. It was as if the lights were slowly turning on. And then, oh *then* came the most glorious sight I'd ever seen. We stopped running and stood looking up. A breeze blew, sweeping away the dust and there it was . . . clear blue sky above like the ocean!

We stared at each other, shocked, both understanding it all now. As I leaned against DNA, he cradled my left arm. "Thank you," I breathed with relief. It was so heavy, now that it had stopped working and its weight was really starting to pull at the flesh of my arm stump and shoulder. I wiped the blood from my nose with my right hand. As I looked up at the sky as I tested *it* out. Yes, I could still see and the pomegranate of eyes could still see me. This was even a surprise to them. We sat down right there on the hard packed sand. A breeze blowing. We stared into each other's eyes letting the sunshine heat the facts into our spirits: The Red Eye was a disaster. However, it was not a *natural* one. It had been manmade. "Now I *truly* understand why you were their worst nightmare," DNA said.

Fifteen minutes later, a small drone whirred to us and

dropped two bottles of water and a sunflower with an oily sack full of freshly fried sweet plantain tied to its thick stem. We drank and ate right there in the desert sun. I sniffed the sunflower. The water washed the blood from my mouth, the plantain made me forget it was ever there and the sunflower smelled beautiful. It was a better meal than the one I'd planned back in Abuja. It was all I wanted.

═══

And in several big cities in a country far far away, the lights went out.

ACKNOWLEDGMENTS

***Noor* was a novel that** came to me out of nowhere. I walked out of Nigeria's Murtala Muhammed International Airport in 2017, inhaled the Lagos air and, BOOM, the first scene rushed into my head like a spirit . . . and AO started talking to me. I sat down right there on the central median bench while I was waiting for my ride to pick me up and wrote the first few paragraphs.

This was a novel I wrote quietly without telling anyone about it but my daughter Anyaugo. And she championed me all the way through. So I'd like to thank Anyaugo first and foremost for being my audience and keeping me focused on what was most important in the story. In 2019, I traveled to Ouarzazate, Morocco with my daughter to visit the largest solar plant in Africa, the Noor Solar Complex. The site director Mustafa Sellam spent the day showing us around and by the time we left, I understood that there was power and clean energy to be harvested in African deserts. The Noor Solar Complex was where the title for this novel came from and its innovation was one of the foundations.

Thank you to writer Chris Abani for offering his deep knowledge of the cultures and politics in the northern region of Nigeria. Thank you to my editor Betsy Wollheim for loving this novel from the moment she read it. A hearty thanks to

Greg Ruth for his epic rendering of AO on the cover. Greg and I talk extensively about my characters before he draws them, so he packed a lot into that image. Thank you to graphic designer Jim Tierney for that awesome font on the cover. Thank you to my literary agent Donald Maass for his streamlining feedback.

Lastly, I'd like to thank that haboob I experienced in Phoenix, Arizona for inspiring my writer's mind to imagine a city within dust and wind.